jet-setting

Thank you for your support. May the pages ahead inspire you to connect w/ your life lessons.

Cheers to life, love & lessons ♡

Tiera Nacole

Lesson

Gifted

Away

TIERA NACOLE

Lesson Gifted Away

Published by Novel Nikki

Copyright © 2018 by Tiera "Tiera Nacole" Gilder

All rights reserved.

ISBN-13: 978-1-7322196-0-1

Cover by Eddy and Christyn Fobbs with Creatif Design Studio, www.creatif-ds.com

Edits and interior design by Jessica Tilles www.twasolutions.com

I dedicate this book to every woman who was audacious enough to honor her inner Voice and follow Truth, regardless of fears lurking presence. Thank you for choosing to give your voice life, even when silence sounded more alluring. Your acts of courage serve as precious life lessons for those who will one day travel a similar path.

Lastly, in remembrance of guilt and shame may they never live beyond the boundaries of our memories. Rot In Peace (RIP)

Note From the Author

Since I can remember, I've always been a lover of words and bringing them to life. I knew one day I would be privileged to write a novel, but I battled with *when*. Oftentimes, I felt the nudge to let my fingers dance along the keyboard, but I let fear intimidate me. Inconveniences, insecurities, and procrastination talked me out of writing. Or so they thought… I've come to realize that God had more life for me to live before I could write such a profound story. The reality of God choosing me to author *Lesson Gifted Away* leaves me in awe. God, thank you for being patient, gentle, merciful, and gracious towards me throughout this process. This was a divinely orchestrated moment that you fashioned just for me. Trusting Your process and surrendering to Your timing have been two of my greatest life lessons. Prayerfully, we will embark on another literary adventure, and I promise to be a better apprentice ☺ I love you, God!

To my Literary Warriors, thank you for reading my premature and grammatically challenged diamond in the rough. When I felt the most vulnerable, you saw the potential of my work and helped me shape it into a gem. At times when uncertainty and fear tried to deceive me, your constructive feedback, support, and love helped me see the truth. Daisy Abcede, Monica Benson, Marquise Elder, Nichole Flanagan, Spencer Foreman, Natasha Frazier, Richard Fulk, Marshana Gilder, Mary Gilder, Yvonne Hollis (my granny), Connie Jacobs, Tana McKelvey, Geralyn Mosely, and Jeanette Westin, the completion of Lesson Gifted away is an extension of my gratitude to you. My editor, Jessica Tilles, you are absolutely remarkable. The valuable wisdom and expertise you bestowed turned my manuscript into a novel! Eddy and Christyn Fobbs, founders of Creatif Design Studio, the world has yet to see the depth of your creative genius. Thank you for creating a cover that illustrates the heart of my story!

To my Village of Family, Friends, and Ancestors, because of you, Lesson Gifted Away made it from my heart to paper! From before my conception to this moment, your prayers, mentorship, correction, guidance, discipline, and precious love ordered my steps and gave me the courage to live beyond my vision. Many of our shared experiences are echoed in the life lessons gifted away in my novel. Words cannot begin to express the depth of my gratitude.

A special word of love to my parents, Mary and Rayford Gilder, and my sister, MarShana Gilder. Mom and Dad, your shared wisdom, encouragement and guidance have been my tools for survival. You loved me when I didn't know how to love myself and believed in me when my faith was shaken. Thank you for granting me glimpses of God's love through you. Sissy, you are my numero uno diva, best friend, and literary role model. As established authors, I thank you and mom for coaching me with your literary love. You both have a fierce talent and authenticity that inspire me!

To my new friend, Kendall Marie Johnson, thank you for choosing me to tell your story. Creating your character and unveiling your truths has been an adventure of self-exploration, patience, faith, and love. Your life lessons have inspired me and become my own. To share them with the world is a gift I will always treasure.

Lastly, to you, thank you for choosing *Lesson Gifted Away*. As you travel through the pages, may you be challenged, inspired, and empowered to trust your journey and identify the many lessons life has gifted you. Once revealed, I dare you to share them with the world.

Cheers to Life, Lessons, and Love,

Tiera Nacole

In memory of my "crazy, sexy, cool" friend, confidant, and spiritual advisor, SonJa Tucker, aka Mother Earth. I'm so grateful to be one of the many souls you profoundly touched. My dear, if Heaven ever decides to open for visiting hours, you will be one of the first I visit. Love you.

"To die and it be as though you never lived will be the legacy of those who chose fear; however, to die and it be as though you live forever will be the legacy of those who chose faith."

– Tiera Nacole

My Current Situation

What... Wait... What... Car accident? Brain trauma? Emergency surgery? Respirator? DNR? Hospice? What's going on? Wait, wait, wait! Hello? Please, can anybody, somebody hear me? WAIT!

Twenty-five days, fifteen hours, and thirteen minutes later, I am motionless in a hospital bed, unable to speak, move, or open my eyes; all modes of communication with the world are non-existent, at least for me. With my heightened sense of hearing, the clock on the wall tortures me as it celebrates each second of my slow demise. Offended by the clocks mockery of my situation, my grasp of time is dependent on nurses coming into my room for shift change at 7:00 a.m. and 7:00 p.m. Now the doctors, they are a lost cause. With their erratic schedules, relying on them for timekeeping purposes is useless. As for entertainment, the hospital staff fills me on more raunchy affairs and juicy medical gossip than one could ever gather from watching *Grey's Anatomy*. Minus the camcorder and film crew, yours truly is literally in a medical soap opera, cast to play dead, which is an effortless task for me.

When the soap opera breaks for a commercial and all beloved visitors leave, I return to the reality of being a hostage in a lifeless-like body. With no control over my bowels and hair needing to be deep-conditioned, surely my unibrow has reared its ugly head. The idea of no lip-gloss or mascara is utterly disturbing, not that I consider myself vain. However, complaining is not an option. I did this! All the blame for my current condition is *my* fault and I must live with it.

Before I spiral deeper into my daily hour of self-pity, the only voice that could ease my tearless cries interrupts me.

"Kendall Marie. Hey, not sure if you can even hear me."

Yes! Oh my gosh, Carvin! I'm alive! Please touch me. Kiss me. I feel like I've been buried alive and I'm so hungry.

Next in line to tasting Carvin's lips, my inner Big Girl yearns for him to feed her some rolled tacos, peach cobbler, gumbo, yellow curry chicken, lumpia, collard greens, bread pudding... My thoughts ramble away from Carvin's presence, as I fantasize about yanking out this feeding tube and giving in to Big Girl's avaricious appetite.

"Damn it, Kendall! How could you do this to me? To us! I want to hate you, Lord knows I do. Not only did you hurt me, but you devastated your family. And you—" Before diving off the cliff of truth, Carvin caught his last words and replaced them with a heavy sigh.

I'm so sorry, Carvin. I'm so sorry! I love you. I need you not to give up on me. On us... Please!

Carvin continued with his rant, seeming unmoved by my silent stillness. "I blame myself even more because I ignored the signs. I should have known, I should have listened, I should have... I probably should have left a long time ago... But, that's on me. I hoped my love was enough—"

Baby, don't say that! Carvin, please don't go... Please, oh please... I need you! Carvin, don't leave me like this! God, please give him a sign that I'm still here.

Carvin adjusts the blinds of the only window in my room, probably hoping the peeking rays from the sun will penetrate the dense cloud between us. However, the tone in the words that follow proves his attempts are futile.

"I can't do this, not after what you did to yourself and... I loved you and you go do this!" Carvin pauses, as if waiting for me to counter and prove his accusations are wrong. The loud chime of the telemetry machine signaling the nurse to check my heart rate probably reminds him of the medical condition holding me under duress. Leaning in closer, he whispers, "If you can hear me, why would you hurt us like this? Damn, Kendall! You chose to do this over what we had!" Pulling away, he kicks the trash can near my bed as he attempts to control himself. "I really hope you've learned a valuable life lesson. I know I have. God help me... Good bye, Kendall Marie!"

Carvin, you don't mean that. Carvin! Wait, no. Please come back. I'm alive. I will fix this. PLEASE, don't leave me. You don't understand; it's not what you think... Trust me, as soon as I... As soon as I...

Then it hits me. With my spirit imprisoned by this hollow shell of a body, "as soon as I" may never come. Yes, I have learned more valuable life lessons than Carvin could ever know. Many of them I agree with. Life lessons that, if blessed with another chance, I would gift to anyone and everyone that would listen. However, the stark reality is that I already cashed in on my second chance and failed.

The slamming door torments me, reminding me that my fiancé is gone, taking with him my dreams of a "happily ever after." Carvin never curses at me or calls me by my first and middle names. Hearing him berate me with verbal slurs kills me beyond the death I'm trying to escape. Several more times, my thoughts scream out his name, hoping the angels will escort him back to my bedside. Yet, my pleas will not travel from my heart to my mouth. If I can cry, I will, but my body is non-reactive.

Now alone with the melodic chime of the respirator, I'm reminded of the weight of Guilt as it proceeds to comfort me. Guilt has not only been consistently present throughout my life these past few years, but has remained at my bedside since the accident. Although not my preferred company, I now appreciate its loyalty. My only constant companion has made reminding me of my indiscretions its fee for our friendship. Being lonely and afraid, I accept Guilt's terms. As it reminds me of my many mistakes, something else in me allows me to see the lessons in them. Although not always easy, given Guilt is extremely jealous and territorial, the lessons have proven resilient. As long as I am open to receive them, I am able to perceive them, of which Guilt has no control over.

Although we have never met, I am sure you can find facets of me in you. We all have loved, hurt, cried, laughed, and failed. Ironically, the one person I loved the most I failed the greatest. Knowing there is nothing I can do about it is the most paralyzing pain. My last resort toward any moral amends would be to share my treasure chest of life lessons with you. That way, if I die, it will not be as though I never lived; you can carry my legacy of lessons forward.

Given we are pages apart, your decision to proceed will be validated if you allow the lessons of my life to touch yours.

So, here it goes...

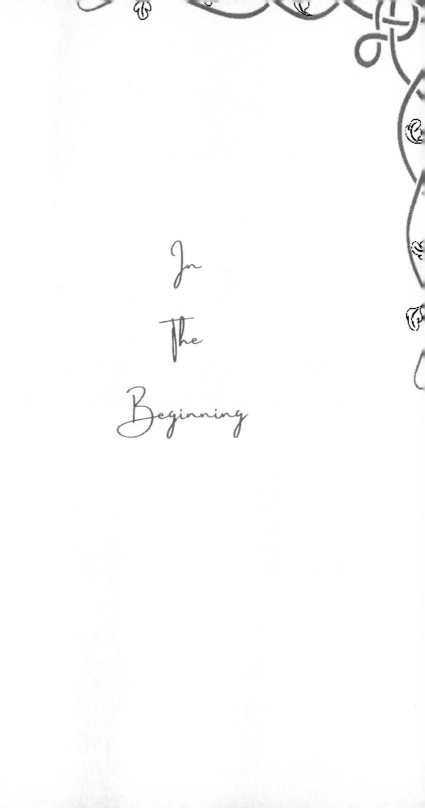

In

The

Beginning

One

To share my life without divulging some of the insanely embarrassing moments of my childhood would be safe for me and unfair to you. So, before I dive too deep into the present, let me give you a sneak peek at the younger, more awkward me.

Growing up, when it came to talking, I was guaranteed to take home the gold. Not necessarily due to quality, but most found the quantity extreme. I wasn't the cutest kid on the block, nor could I rely on my athletic talent to overshadow my awkward gait and wayward hair. Like any pre-teen trying to circumvent the wrath of bullying, I resorted to talking trash. I would talk trash about trash if that meant avoiding ridicule behind being super skinny, with teeth larger than Texas and more widely spread.

In contrast, my best friend, Carrie, was beautiful, bubbly, and naïve. We first met in elementary school at a fifth-grade Halloween dance my parents forced me to attend with my younger brother, Kenton. Afraid the strobe lighting would expose my ugly, sulking in a dark corner near the auditorium exit was my refuge. Unsolicited, Carrie floated toward me, asking why I wasn't dancing and, of course, I told an outrageous lie.

"Who me? Girl, please! I would hate to shame you all. I used to be a background dancer for Immature and Brandy…"

Hoping to distract her with lies, I started doing the moonwalk on the newly polished wood floors.

To my surprise, her gullibility misled her. "Wow, I love Immature and Brandy. How cool! Ya have to show me some of ya moves." Her family roots were in New Orleans, Louisiana, which explained her heavy Cajun accent; a complete contrast to my proper dialect.

Fortunately, I did know their moves. Although I had never been a background dancer for anyone, I watched enough BET to nail MC Hammer in any dance battle. After a little pleading and begging from Carrie, I agreed to show her a few of my moves. Not only could she not dance, I was astonished she was pigeon-toed, too. From that moment on, we were inseparable.

That next year, we both made the jump to middle school. Intimidated by the middle school crowd, we relied on each other for courage, comfort, and friendship. We ate lunch together, studied together, and even daydreamed about the eighth-grade jocks together. Carrie was the first friend who made me feel comfortable in my awkward skin. No longer did I feel like I had to hide behind my bad attitude to mask my imperfections.

By the dawn of high school, our lunch gatherings, study sessions, and daydreaming subsided. Unlike me, Carrie garnered further courage and popularity from a trait that was currently extinct to me—beauty. By the middle of ninth grade, our friendship had simmered down to sporadic study sessions and silent walks to the bus stop. Was I jealous? Of course, I was! However, the hurt and anger by her dismissal of our friendship were my greatest hurdles to overcome. The one person who I had shared all my secrets and dreams with was now trading me in for romps in the bathroom with pubescent athletes and lunch with the popular girls.

Not knowing how to seek revenge, I was ecstatic when the universe presented me with what I perceived as the perfect opportunity. Although ridiculing my friend went against my teenaged moral compass, I was immature and desperate for payback.

One afternoon, prior to fifth-period biology lab, I decided to ditch class and go to the local corner store for Lemonheads, Flamin' Hot Cheetos, and a red soda. Although ditching could result in my suspension, I found the risk of being caught exhilarating. With a mouthful of Cheetos and soda, I discreetly dashed back toward the obscure alley behind the convenience store, hoping to make it in time for my next class. As I was turning into the alley, I heard whispering and giggling by the dumpster. Holding my breath to avoid making a sound and inhaling the rancid fumes of yesterday's trash, I slowly crept forward. As I peeked around the disheveled pile of black trash bags, a loud shriek greeted me. To my horror, Carrie was on her knees and one of the boys we used to daydream about was zipping up his jeans.

"Oh! Uh, hey, Ken, what ya doing here? Umm, I was on my way to class, too." Carrie's words stuttered out as she wiped her mouth, never once allowing our eyes to lock.

Appalled that she would play me for a fool, I asked, without hesitation, "Really, while on your knees? Let me guess, you're trying to get a *head* start on next year's Human Anatomy lab?" Looking over the rim of my shades, I placed extra emphasis on *head*.

Carrie never answered, but the tears and shock drowning her eyes spoke volumes. Even more astonishing was the boy's response. Obviously, he cared little about her or her reputation.

"Dang, Kendall, that was a good one. Look, I gotta go to practice. I'll catch you later, Carrie. Oh, and thanks." He chuckled, shaking his head while he jogged down the alley back to campus.

With nothing more to say, I followed suit, leaving Carrie to wallow in her embarrassment.

Now you would think that would be enough, but the greed of revenge has a way of possessing us in order to feed its relentless hunger. I headed toward sixth period, internally gloating over my victory. I had managed to humiliate the girl who was once my best friend and, in the process, receive a compliment from the boy I had been drooling over all semester.

Fortunately, the bell rang just as I walked into my geometry class. Out of breath from running, I fumbled to situate myself at my desk, taking out my scientific calculator and protractor.

My teacher, Ms. Jones, announced my arrival. "Hi, Kendall, welcome to class. Students, do any of you happen to know where Carrie is?"

Yes! I think, as this is another opportunity for me to defame her name and feed my greed. Without any thought or consideration of the consequences, my hand shot up and the words raced forward. "Yeah, she's behind the corner store, fooling around with some boy!"

Immediately, some of my classmates erupted in laughter and others whispered among themselves about the truth of my accusations.

"Class, please quiet down!" Ms. Jones paused as she collected her thoughts and then continued. "Kendall, I presume your knowing where Miss Carrie is would explain why you also were not present in fifth-period biology lab?"

My chest immediately closed in on me, as my heart frantically tried to beat its way out. What was I thinking? How could I have been so impulsively stupid! Not only did Ms. Jones teach geometry class, she also substituted that day for my biology teacher. All I could do was stare at her, terrified by the sinking hole I had just dug for myself.

"Am I also to assume the answer I need is in your sudden silence?"

She was right. I continued to respond with my quiet guilt and humiliation, unable to tear my eyes from her slanted stare.

"Well, with that said, students, please review exercises one through five. I will give a quiz when I return. Kendall, please gather all of your items and follow me to Principal Wilson's office."

The walk to the principal's office felt like the longest walk ever, despite being just a few doors away. Not only did Principal Wilson suspend me for the rest of the week, my parents whooped and punished me. Carrie was also suspended, but due to the level of embarrassment, her parents withdrew her and enrolled her in a high school across town.

As would be expected, our friendship plummeted to ashes after that incident. It was years later, in college, that we re-established our sisterhood as Sorors. With the passing of time and the healing of hurts, we could now reminisce and laugh at her promiscuous naiveté and my self-inflicted suspension.

During my senior year in college, I was invited by my high school to speak to the graduating class about college preparation and overcoming peer pressure. Given my tumultuous high school journey turned college success story, I was excited to share wisdom. During that visit, I ran into Ms. Jones, who immediately brought up that dreadful day in her class.

"You know what, Kendall? If it weren't for your Freudian slip, I would have never realized you had ditched fifth period. To my fault, I had forgotten to take attendance. When you spoke up, I immediately thought, 'How would you know about that?' And then, I realized I didn't recall seeing you in biology lab."

"Wait, you mean to tell me if I had kept quiet I could have dodged one of the worst butt whoopings I ever received? Wow.

In my angst to get back at Carrie, I had forgotten that you were teaching fifth and sixth periods that day. She still teases me about that to this day."

Heading to our cars on this particular sunny afternoon, we stopped in the middle of the school parking lot and embraced. "Well, don't be too hard on yourself. I actually use your story as an example of a lesson I learned years ago."

"And, how did my embarrassment inspire you?"

Ms. Jones chuckled under her breath as she searched through her purse for her keys. "Shut up and be still. In life, God doesn't need a co-pilot, Kendall. As the Bible eloquently instructs, be swift to hear, slow to speak, and slow to anger. Every sophisticated lady should practice this."

Up to that point, my take away from that experience was to leave vengeance to God. I projected the repercussions on Carrie, as if my punishment was a result of her indiscretions. Ms. Jones helped me realize I was the major culprit. My haste for revenge caused me to trip over my own deceit, creating more pain and humiliation for the both of us. All I could do was thank God for showing grace on my renewed friendship with Carrie.

From that day forward, I took steps toward being more mindful of my words and the intentions behind my actions. As you shall soon see, I was not always successful, but I certainly tried.

 Be swift to hear, slow to speak, and slow to anger. James 1:19

 The predator desperate for revenge will become prey to its own greed.

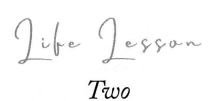

Life Lesson

Two

One might speculate the loss of my "best friend forever" would have humbled me early on. To be honest, the guilt did keep me reclusive for the first half of high school. That, and the fact my untamed teeth kept potential suitors away. However, during my junior year, I blossomed in a way that dramatically reshaped my life and the life of those around me.

Dr. Crane, our family dentist, smiled at me as I sauntered around in her office like a peacock, trying to seduce my next lover. For most young girls, turning sixteen would gift them with their first date, a sweet sixteen party, or possibly their first car. For me, my sixteenth birthday brought me freedom. The summer before eleventh grade, Dr. Crane freed my mouth from the shackles of braces, allowing my newly manicured teeth to show off their pearly perfection. I was ecstatic! The ugly duckling had blossomed into the Swan Princess, and now all I wanted was my prince.

For the past sixteen years, the only kisses I received from the opposite sex were from Dad and Grandpa. I had yet to experience the heart warming, toe-curling, romantic rush from tasting the kiss of a crush. Since the onset of my menstrual

13

cycle, I had a few sexual encounters within the realm of my dreams, but the extent of that pleasure never crossed over into reality. When I was about to reach the climax I yearned for, the real world always had a way of waking me up.

Secretly, I made it my mission to use my new beauty to bait and hook the hottest senior varsity football player, Davis Crews. During the remainder of my summer break, I underwent external reconstruction. I adorned my bathroom drawers with mascara, lipsticks, eye shadows, and foundation. Heels, sandals, skorts, snug jeans, and fitted blouses decorated my closet. I ditched my ponytail for cascading braids, hoping their swaying length would capture his heart.

Fast forward, the first day of junior year arrived and I was excited to premiere my new, promiscuous look. I recall waking up before the sun to primp my hair, beautify my face, and shave my legs. Once dressed to my satisfaction, I accented my look with my favorite Victoria's Secret body spray: Strawberries and Champagne.

As I walked into the kitchen to get some breakfast, my annoying younger brother, Kenton, laughed loudly. "Ken, what in the hell are you wearing? *Dang,* dude, you look like Homey the Clown did your hair and Ray Charles did your makeup!"

"Go play with yourself, Kenton!" I retorted, while slyly throwing him the middle finger behind Mom's back.

Our mother abruptly quieted our bickering. "Kenton, if I have to tell you one more time to be mindful of your words, I will beat you upside the head like Homey the Clown. Now turn around in your seat, eat, and shut up!"

She rolled her eyes at my brother and diverted her piercing eyes toward me. "And, Kendall Marie, I will not tolerate your inappropriate remarks either. It's way too early for all this nonsense." She stared at me for a moment before she continued. "Now, what in the hell did you slather on your face? Sweetie, you don't need all of that makeup masking your natural beauty. And, your hair, I should have never allowed you to put that mess in your head. I'm so distracted by all this stuff you have going on." Mom's head-to-toe inspection felt more like an autopsy. To avoid her eyes from cutting me any deeper, I walked to the other side of the breakfast bar.

"And that perfume. I could smell you coming down the stairs. You know how sensitive your father's allergies are, my goodness! Baby, come back over here and turn around for me." I reluctantly walked back toward her, my eyes sweeping the floor as I slowly turned around like the ballerina in my jewelry box. "Oh no! Sweetie, I can see the crack of your behind!"

My brother spat out his cereal as he erupted in laughter.

"Kenton, what did I say? Better yet, you're excused from the table. Go upstairs and grab your bag so I can drop you off at school."

"But, Ma, I told you she looks like—"

"Boy, did I stutter? Go get your bag… Now! Brush your teeth, too. I'm sure you didn't do that!"

My brother sulked upstairs, mumbling under his breath, eager to have the last word, but too cowardice to test Mom further.

"Kendall, I assume your father hasn't seen you because he would have summoned you to your room and sought me for counsel." Mom stopped mixing her homemade pancake batter and looked at me through desperate, questioning eyes. "Sweetheart, what's this all about? You're already a naturally pretty girl. Since you got your braces off, I notice you have been consumed with how you look. You spend all of your time staring at yourself in the mirror, you wear makeup twenty-four-seven, your clothes are revealing, and your attitude has gotten you in more trouble this summer than it has over the past sixteen years. Do you realize the type of attention you will attract, leaving nothing to the imagination? Definitely not the type you deserve."

As always, my mouth was my greatest enemy. "Okay and... what's wrong with that?"

Clearly baffled by my lack of tact, Mom put her hands on her hips, smiled, and looked toward the staircase. "Baby! Please come downstairs, I want to show you something." She then peered back at me, slowly looking me up and down. Once we locked eyes again, she handed me a plate of food and motioned for me to sit down at the kitchen table, never once allowing the smirk to leave her face. She turned back toward the stove and continued frying bacon and mixing batter. Mom was naturally loquacious and sassy, so I found her silence nerve-racking.

Dad came whistling down the stairs, kissed Mom on the lips, and proceeded to embrace her petite curves with his muscular six-foot frame. It was obvious, from her girlish giggles, that he was whispering some explicit secrets that neither wanted me to hear. One thing I could never deny was the genuine love and affection my parents had for one another. After what felt like an eternity, Dad turned around, shocked to find me unenthusiastically watching their display.

"Oh hey, Kendall, I didn't realize you were down here." Dad immediately walked over and gave me a loving kiss on the forehead. "Are you ready for school, Miss Lady?"

"I don't know, ask Mom." Where all of this courage was coming from, I still don't know. Although my mouth ran away from me at times, I had always been very respectful toward my parents. With my new face and wardrobe, I felt like my outer beauty was all the courage I needed, or so I thought.

Without turning away from the stove, Mom responded, "Kendall Marie, get up and show your dad how gorgeous you look."

I knew it. She was setting me up. The fact that she was addressing me by my first and middle name was evidence of the bomb waiting to explode. Afraid that if I didn't obey I would be blanketed in hot bacon grease, I stood up and slowly walked toward Dad. He stepped back and gave me a once over, spending extra time observing my face.

"Turn around for your dad, Kendall Marie," Mom added, still not turning away from the stove. Once I finished my pitiful pivot, she demanded, "Now go sit back down, please," never once removing her gaze from the sizzling skillet.

Once seated, Mom and Dad locked eyes. As they always did, they proceeded to have a mental conversation with one another. No words were exchanged, just unbroken eye contact and silence. Without breaking their gaze, Mom said, "So, what do you think? Does your baby girl look beautiful for her first day of eleventh grade?"

Dad smiled at Mom, never breaking eye contact. "Of course, she does." By this time, I was tired of their mental tango. Finally, Dad must have felt my anguish because he looked at me and said, "Sweetheart, go get your things so I can take you to school."

Stuffing the last two pieces of bacon in my mouth, I hugged Dad, thankful that he always seemed to have my back. I skipped upstairs feeling triumphant that I finally dodged Mom's efforts to control me.

Halfway up the stairs, Dad interrupted my euphoria by yelling, "And, Kendall, be sure to wash that mess off your face, put on a longer skirt, and button your shirt up all the way."

SERIOUSLY!

Courage found by wearing excess makeup, revealing clothes, and/or being disrespectful to others is always fleeting. This false sense of courage will lead you into the lion's den, only to leave you stranded.

If left unchecked, unresolved pain and insecurities can be a source of hurt for you and those you love.

Embrace your natural beauty

Three

Over the next several months, I had a love affair with arrogance and pride. My attitude toward my parents grew more noxious and disrespectful, while my brother and I became archenemies. Whenever my dad dropped me off at school, I would rush into the girl's restroom and transform into my alter ego. Realizing my newfound popularity was directly related to my risqué attire and made-up face, I did what any naïve girl would do to garner more attention, I amped up the intensity.

The amount of attention I received from the star athletes was surreal; I relished in it. The greatest reward for my rebellion was the day Davis invited me to hang out after his game. The excitement alone almost stopped my heart. My initial reaction was to decline so that I could study for my AP Chemistry exam, but that decision was short lived.

"Wow! I mean, I guess, I would like that. But, I kinda need to study, so I probably—"

"Come on, baby! You gotta come out. Your fine ass can be my sweet, good luck charm! With you there, I'm bound to win." He licked his luscious lips, as he leaned over and brushed them up against my ear. "Besides, I'm really diggin' you. I've been feelin' you for hella years, Ken."

I overlooked the fact that he just transferred to my school last semester, so clearly he's only known of my existence for less than a year. His curly hair, sleepy eyes, and the throbbing sensation between my thighs erased all of my common sense and I softly responded, "Wow, really? Okay, sure."

To diminish my parents' suspicion, my study partner turned BFF, Jasmine, agreed to escort me to the game in her new car. As usual, I left home looking like Mary Poppins, but as soon as I got to school, I went to the restroom and came out looking like Mary Magdalene.

"Ummm, oh wow! Lord, where has my innocent friend gone? I rebuke that short skirt, your tight tank top, and that mask of makeup!" Jasmine mocked while lifting her eyes and hands to Heaven for a divine answer.

I laughed, slapping her on the arm. "Jasmine, stop being so dramatic! You didn't know? I'm about to go get my man!"

"Oh, okay. You do know he's only interested in screwing you, right? Otherwise, he would have approached you last semester. Think about it, he never even looked your way until your booty and titties started talking to him."

I rolled my eyes at Jasmine. "Whatever, he really likes me. He told me how he's been feeling me since he got here!"

The truth of the matter was that Jas was right. Sadly, my pride wouldn't let me admit it. Last year, I used to intentionally walk by him or say *hi*, and he never once acknowledged me. As much as I knew he only wanted my body, I hoped that if he really got to know me he would fall in love with my mind, too. I was hopeful that I could change him, even if that meant using my body as bait.

After the game was over, I told Jasmine to wait for me in her car while I spent some alone time with Davis. Jasmine was hesitant. However, after much pleading, she obliged, but not after threatening to come find me in exactly an hour. After I pinky promised to return to her car in sixty minutes or less, we parted ways.

Davis and I met outside of the boy's locker room and headed toward the back of the gym. The entire time we walked, he ranted and complained about how they would have won if it weren't for Coach Harper taking him out of the game. Uninterested, I resorted to daydreaming about the possibility of him kissing me. I assume he saw my dwindling interest because he grabbed me and started passionately kissing me up against a flickering light post. I melted.

"I have something else you'll enjoy." He stepped closer, allowing the salty soap fragrance of his skin to invade my nostrils. His left hand slowly slithered up my skirt as his right hand led my trembling fingers toward the hardness inside his shorts. "Lace panties, my favorite. You don't mind if I touch them, do you?" He smirked, as he proceeded to massage my inner thigh.

"Huh?" I abruptly pulled myself away from him, shyly laughing at his aggressive humor. "Ha. Boy, you're crazy."

Without warning, Davis yanked me closer, forcefully kissing me on the neck as his rough hands invaded the privacy between my thighs. "Like I said, I've been feeling you for years and I want to see if what lies under your skirt feels as good as you smell! Come on, baby, just let me play with it for a little bit."

I immediately panicked, feeling torn. On one hand, I was strangely turned on by his forceful desire for me, but on the other hand, I feared what might follow.

"Look, Davis, um, I better go. Jasmine is probably looking for me. Besides, I really need to study."

"Yeah, right! Study what?" He stopped kissing me to give me a side eyed look. "Look, stop playing hard to get. The way you flaunt your half-dressed ass around school, it's clear you ain't studying nothing but this dick! Now take them off!" Davis yanked my arm to pull me closer as he started tearing at my panties.

21

"Excuse me! Let my arm go, Davis! I'm not playing with you; leave me the hell alone! I'm going home. You're crazy! Please stop! No. No!"

As much as I tried to fight him off, my strength was no comparison to his muscles of adrenaline and determination. The next thing I know, he violently reduced me to a concubine behind the gym. The salt of his sweat dissolved the scent of my body spray; my mascara and eye shadow rinsed away by my tears, and my virginity broken by his force. He raped me.

After stealing my innocence, Davis pulled up his pants, kissed me on the forehead, and walked away, leaving me to wallow in my misery. Minutes later, I heard Jasmine yelling my name, but I couldn't muster up the strength to respond. Finally, she found me, and from the look of terror on her face, I knew my scars were visible. Overcome with the guilt that I had solicited this punishment because of my revealing wardrobe, I put the blame on myself. Jasmine, of course, wouldn't buy it. I attempted to swear her to secrecy, begging her not to tell my parents or anyone else, but she wasn't having it.

"Kendall, are you freaking kidding me?" she exclaimed. "You. Were. Raped. Now you expect me to keep quiet? You're crazy!" Jas shot back as she assisted with buttoning the few buttons clinging to my torn blouse.

"He didn't mean it, Jas. Look at how I've been dressing and behaving. He was right; my actions brought this on. My mom was right. Oh my God, my mom was so right!" A tsunami of tears broke through. Jasmine grabbed me and did her best to console me, but my shame was so thick I couldn't feel her comfort.

"Oh Kendall. Girl, this is not your fault. No one should ever be a victim of some creep violating them. I don't care how skimpy you dress or how much makeup you wear, rape is a brutal breach of your human rights!"

"Why would he do this to me, Jasmine? Why? I said no over and over and over! It was like my resistance enraged him more," I bellowed between sobs.

"What a shitty bastard! I'm so sorry I wasn't here for you. I wish I would've followed my intuition. Look, we gotta go home, Kendall. We have to tell your parents so they can get you to a hospital and call the police." Jas proceeded to pull me forward as I yanked my arm away.

"No!" All I heard was *tell my parents* and *call the police.* "Jasmine, I'm not telling my parents and I am definitely not calling the police!"

"Okay, then I will!"

"Jasmine! No!" I screamed as I attempted to will my body up from the cold cement, this time motioning for her assistance.

"Look, Kendall, either you tell your parents or I will. He raped you! I need you to understand that. This mess was not some consensual quickie! He raped you and you're going to let him get away with that? Hell no! If not for yourself, at least tell so that he doesn't do it to someone else!"

Jasmine was right. I just wasn't ready to reveal this to my parents. I was still trying to break through my own fog of pain. What I needed was a hot shower and time to sort through my thoughts. I knew I had to make some type of deal with Jasmine, or else she would rush straight to my parents and break the silence. Eventually, I would tell them, just not as quick as she would have preferred.

"You're right. I just need a moment to sort through all of this. I'm so confused," I cried out, "just give me a moment, Jasmine. Okay. I promise I will tell them. Can I stay with you tonight? I can't face them right now, I can barely face myself."

Jasmine stared at me, looking for any hints that I might break the promise that I just made to her. When she finally felt comfortable that my promise was authentic, she agreed to take me to her house.

A woman's worth is not defined by how she looks or dresses, but by how she values herself.

Rape is and always will be an inexcusable act of violence—it's not your fault.

Honor your mother and father. One day the wisdom behind their words just might be your saving grace.

Four

*E*ight weeks went by and I had yet to reveal to my parents what happened. With Jasmine barking threats to say something if I didn't, I knew I had to open up fast. But, I was terrified.

When at school, I made every effort to avoid Davis. Memorizing his schedule made it easy for me to dodge him. The one time I did run into him, he acted as if nothing ever happened. I tried to ignore his attempts to get my attention, and rushed into the restroom where I wept profusely. When I wasn't at school or studying, I reminisced over the pain I had caused Carrie and the crucifixion she suffered behind my judgment. I ridiculed her for pimping her beauty for attention, never imagining a couple years later I would indulge in similar acts. Except my skimpy behavior had and would result in far more dire consequences. I was hurting so bad, and the worst part is that I didn't have the courage to tell anyone.

As always, life has a way of forcing courage upon you. When you wait for courage to find you, most times, it's not in the most pleasant way.

Courage found me feeling extremely fatigued and nauseas, barely able to keep anything down. With the stress of final exams and the agony of rape hovering over me, I figured my physical symptoms were a direct result. Mom, being a nurturer, was worried and immediately made me a doctor's appointment.

The memory of that day is so easily retrievable. On that cold and rainy Friday morning, Mom had just finished making her famous grits casserole and pancakes. Before I could even savor the first bite, yesterday's dinner invaded my taste buds, forcing its way onto the kitchen table. Mom immediately canceled her morning office hours and rushed me to our local Primary Care Physician's office.

After meeting with Dr. Kaiser, we sat in the paisley themed, cozy waiting area. Completely exhausted from vomiting multiple times on the drive to the doctor's office, I rested my limp body up against Mom for additional support.

After fifteen minutes of wrestling with nausea and sweat, I had finally found a semi-comfortable position with my legs draped across two chairs and my head propped up against the cold, wallpapered wall. Unfortunately, my relief was startled when Dr. Kaiser summoned us back into her office.

"Mrs. Jones, do you mind if I speak with you and Kendall in my office?"

Mom looked at me and then back at Dr. Kaiser. "Uh, sure. Of course. Is there something wrong, Dr. Kaiser?" We had been sitting in the reception area, waiting for the nurse to bring the prescription to treat what we assumed was the stomach flu. So, when Dr. Kaiser personally requested us to come to her office, we were both slightly confused.

"She's what?" Mom exclaimed.

"I'm pregnant?" I cried out.

"Yes, your pregnancy test came back positive, Kendall. Mrs. Johnson, I would like to get some additional lab work and schedule an ultrasound as soon as possible. When was the last time—"

The walls of the clinic quickly started to close in and suffocate me. I could feel Mom glaring at me. The shape of her lips formed into words, but my heart was beating so loudly, I couldn't hear her.

The car ride home was tense and piercingly silent. The whole time Mom leaned her slender frame into the dashboard, tightly gripping the steering wheel with both hands, as if using it for emotional support. Finally, we pulled up to our house and instead of getting out of the car, she slumped back as she stared straight ahead and let out a loud sigh.

"What did I do, Kendall? Where did we go wrong? Your father and I thought if we enrolled you into the finest schools, showered you with love, and encouraged you to love yourself, you would dodge drugs and sex. Sweetie, what did I do wrong? Why would you ruin your life like this?"

Mom then turned in the seat and looked at me, puffy eyes revealing her wounded spirit. "Pregnant, Kendall, really? I'm so disappointed right now. My God, help me." Mom glanced toward Heaven and then back at me, her sad eyes pleading for an explanation.

I couldn't hold it in anymore. The volcano of truth started boiling up within. Surrounded by Mom's dense cloud of disappointment and the heartbreaking reality of my pregnancy, I could no longer remain silent. As much as I wanted to stay quiet, the truth of my rape erupted in the car.

"I was raped." Tears rushed forward and for the first time in months, I felt the shame of my secret slowly start to rinse away.

The next several months of my life were a whirlwind. After alerting the police, Dad took the lead and sought immediate legal action. To our surprise, due to rape allegations at his previous high school, Davis had moved to Houston from Cleveland, Ohio. Although found evidence was inconclusive and the charges dropped, his mom sent him to live with his father, hoping he could escape his past and start over. My coming forward with my allegations launched an investigation.

Mustering up the strength to give a statement, although liberating, was one of the most trying times of my life. Initially, I refused. Shame convinced me that his egregious act was a deserved reaction to my provocative behavior. My therapist was vital in helping me identify the layers of guilt and shame that I harbored about Carrie, my disrespectful behavior toward my parents, the premarital pregnancy, as well as my insecurities. Once revealed, I gave myself permission to be angry with Davis. During the trial, I relived that tragic night before the jury. As my bloodshot eyes pierced his, daring him to violate me any further with lies, I told it all. It was evident he was uncomfortable, biting his nails and fondling his jumpsuit, only catching my glare when his eyes would come up for air. Weeks following my testimony, the jury found Davis guilty on both accounts of forcible rape and sentenced him to a hefty prison term.

As for me, I carried my son to term. Coupled with the unwavering support of my parents, it was during my therapy sessions that I decided to gift my son up for adoption. On several occasions, my parents asked if they could raise him, but I couldn't bear the thought of looking at him every day and being reminded of Davis. I loved my unborn child too much to subject him to the pain of my past.

After twenty hours of excruciating labor, I met the love of my life. The moment my body screamed out its last push, I let out a shattering cry. It was not because I was relieved, but because I needed more time with him in me and with me. Hearing him release his first wail, the reality of the moment overwhelmed me. The baby angel who had been invading my space for the last nine months was about to leave me forever. Suffocated by this truth, I forgot how to breathe. The nurses rushed to my side and immediately started giving me oxygen, coaching me to relax and breathe. But I couldn't. I was angry, afraid, happy, sad, excited, confused, and ashamed. To know I was utterly in love with a child that I could never have was unbearable.

After several minutes, they succeeded in redirecting my panting to slow, deep breaths. Wiping away my tears, the nurse kindly asked if I was ready to meet my son. I hesitated. Looking away, my eyes landed on my mom. Seated next to me, her eyes met mine and she smiled. She cupped my face with her soft hands and without breaking her stare she gently responded, "Go ahead, Ken, he's yours for this moment. Allow yourself to feel and love him. Otherwise, you may have regrets. Trust me."

I took a deep breath, closing my eyes as I allowed my fear to dissipate with the forced exhale. Still unsure, I inhaled deeply again and slowly exhaled as I opened my eyes. I squeezed Mom's hand as I slowly turned my attention back to the doctor and smiled.

Now looking at the nurse, I softly whispered, "Okay." She gently placed him on my bare chest, guiding my hands to embrace his softness as he wiggled and nuzzled his nose against my swollen breast. Knowing the social worker would be coming to pick him up, my eyes widened, swiftly scanning his toes, fingers, and wrinkled skin for any imperfections. I smiled as his chocolate perfection greeted me. As warm tears lined my eyes, I kissed his tiny fingers, inhaled his scent, and caressed his jet-black curls.

While he drifted off to sleep, I whispered my love in his ears, and hugged him tight. My heart melted between the both of us; I was completely in love with my son.

As the nurse slowly removed him from my embrace, he whined, as if he knew he would never see me again. My heart broke as I pleaded with the nurse for more time, but was reminded his adoptive parents were waiting. Out of empathy, the nurse brought him back over one more time, allowing me to kiss his forehead and inhale his innocence. The gentle knock of the social worker, as she peeked in and nodded to the nurse, signaling the end of our visit, interrupted our bonding moment.

The nurse slowly eased him from my embrace and mouthed, "I'm sorry," as she exited the room, leaving me with only tears to console me to sleep.

Although I was confident that I had made the right decision, the reality of it hurt like hell. I cried and cried and cried and cried during the remainder of my hospital stay. My mother and father remained at my bedside, only leaving to eat or return a call from my brother. Many times, when my father and I were alone, he would wipe away my tears and hug both my hands with his. I relished these private moments together with him. Despite the guilt I felt, he constantly reminded me of how proud he was of me, how inspired he was by my strength and courage. "We will get through this together, sweetheart. Don't worry, baby girl, your Heavenly Father will use your tears to water your seeds of purpose. All things will work together for your good," became his signature statement and I embraced it.

During my last night, I prayed that God would always protect my son, give him parents who will raise him in love, and bless him with a long, prosperous life. In honor of the son I let go, I promised God I would never bring another life into this world.

Instead, vowing to lock my womb away and open up my heart to a better, more successful future. I pledged to never exploit my body for attention, cheapen my self-worth for acceptance, or judge those who find themselves in similar situations. I would begin by setting the standard for how others would treat me, by how I treated myself. That would encompass dignity, respect, and love; but, first I gave myself permission to start forgiving the wounded woman in the mirror.

Think twice before you judge others. Keep living and you might find yourself in their shoes.

True healing starts at the end of self-shaming. Once you deliver yourself from shame, healing will find you.

Life has a way of forcing courage upon you. The problem is, when you wait for courage to find you, most times it's not in the most pleasant way.

God will use your tears to water your seeds of purpose. Your pain is never wasted.

Life Lesson

Five

After several therapy sessions, the promiscuous clothing and pretentious attitude slowly dissipated. With the support of my psychologist and family, the years after my pregnancy, we focused on reforming my image. Once I acknowledged my behavioral and self-confidence issues, forgiveness toward Davis soon followed. Although my final year of high school was weary, I managed to graduate with honors and earn an academic scholarship to Virginia National University. All in all, I succeeded at reallocating my energy toward self-preservation during that time.

This season of preservation continued throughout four exhilarating years of Sorority life, step shows, late night study sessions, and weekend road trips. Dating was an extracurricular activity I frequented during my early years in college, but never allowed myself to engage intimately. Looking back, I recognize it was out of fear of reopening Pandora's box of pain. After working tirelessly to achieve forgiveness of self and Davis, the idea of disturbing that balance frightened me. It wasn't until my Senior year that I slowly gave my heart permission to consider love. Carvin Alexander was my first attempt at this. He was not only chivalrous, but he was also smart and exciting. Looks were not his strongest trait, but he consistently found ways to make me smile. In many ways, he reminded me of my father.

The first several times we did attempt to make love, I couldn't bring myself to relax. The moment he went to remove my clothing or caress my body, I would cringe and stiffen. At times, we would labor through the act and he would willingly stop as my tears coated the pillow. To my surprise, Carvin never displayed agitation or questioned my anxiety, instead reassuring me that he would wait until I was ready. As I became more accustomed to sex as an expression of intimacy, and not a violation, I learned to enjoy it. With time and patience, we established our rhythm and I secretly loved him even more for that.

Post-graduation, I moved back to Houston to pursue my photography goals and Carvin stayed in Virginia to complete his Master's degree in business. For the first year, he made it his priority to see me every other month, all the while constantly serenading me with his thoughts of marriage. Initially I was ecstatic, but my past started to plague my thoughts with guilt and self-shame. Although Carvin embodied all I wanted in love, I felt unworthy. We continued our rendezvous, but the distance and my worries stalled our relationship. Before it could blossom into what God intended, I allowed the worst pesticide to kill it... Fear. As our arguments became more frequent, the romantic gestures and intimate moments disappeared. Through a cowardice voicemail message, intended to break his heart, I succeeded:

Carvin, You may never forgive me and I'm willing to accept that. I will make this short. I can't see you anymore. To be honest, I love you, but I'm not in love with you. I'm sorry. Please don't call.

To my surprise, Carvin met my act of fear with silence; never once trying to change my heart.

To soothe my hurt, I jumped in and out of fleeting situations with men. For reasons that my heart knew, but didn't care to confess, dysfunctional relationships tasted so sweet to me. My dysfunction manifested by settling for men that I knew could never capture my heart. Feeling as if I didn't have the right to choose happiness in love, I subconsciously sought unfulfillment.

After several weekly sessions with my sista-friends, they unofficially diagnosed me with "You-Need-To-Learn-To-Release-The-Regret-From-Your-Past-And-Believe-That-You-Deserve-True-Love" syndrome. Despite the many professional and personal therapy sessions, I believed giving my son away voided my right to experience true love. For reasons I had yet to connect with, the inward affliction would not dissipate.

Empty, broken relationships were the greatest medicine to massage my self-inflicted pain. I became a serial dater, engaging in romantic relationships with men who had no appeal to my spirit. Fine, hell yeah! Nice, sure! Compatible, not really! Carlos, Ronald, Jarvis, Chris, and Zen were all dynamic men. With a father like mine, I wouldn't entertain anything less. However, I allowed myself to lose time in meaningless, unfulfilling relationships because I lacked the courage to take a risk on better.

Have the courage to take a risk on better, even when you don't know what better looks like.

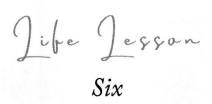

Life Lesson

Six

The more life I experience, the more evident it becomes that God truly has a sense of humor. Just when I accepted I would live a life devoid of true love, courage decided to bully me, forcing me to start removing the layers of fear that I had allowed to intimidate me.

Without further ado, let me introduce you to the last guy I dated before boldness found me.

"Who's your daddy, huh? You love this, don't you, baby? Making you moan and your toes curl! Oh yeah, Daddy takes real good care of his baby!"

"Yes, you do, Papi! Oh, that feels so good!"

One thing I loved more than sex was having my man to wash my hair. It was the epitome of ecstasy. That was one thing James was good at, making sweet love to my scalp. This was his redeeming quality, because in the bed he was worse than a nightmare. As much as I fell asleep during sex with him, if Freddie Krueger were real I would have already been dead on Elm Street. To top it off, the conversation was bland and his humor was unentertaining. With my desire for sex and intriguing conversation, my girlfriends often wondered why I was still stringing James along. The only reason I could give them was loneliness.

One memorable night was when we met up for our monthly night of cocktails and conversations. As usual, we drank more of my life's drama than drinks.

"I'm absolutely dumbfounded. Here you are, this gorgeous, educated, free-spirited diva, and you're settling? What's up, Kendall?" Jasmine blurted out, almost choking on her crown and coke. "Yeah, he may be fine and all, but I never took you to be the shallow type. I guess we learn something new every day, don't we?"

"That's not a fair Jasmine. James is a really great guy. Compared to the wandering-eyed jokers you date, I don't think there's room for you to judge!" I bark, leaning back on my bar stool as I gently tuck a stray curl behind my diamond studded ear.

"Judge? Girl Please. At least you don't have me coming to you asking about how good your sex life is." Jasmine sneered back, playfully rolling her eyes and sucking her teeth.

"What is that supposed to mean?"

"Uh, Kendall, must I remind you? Every time we get together for happy hour, you're begging for the juicy details of my life. If your 'really great guy' was hitting it right, you wouldn't be asking me about mine!"

"You know what Jasmine- Whatever! You can joke about James all you want, but his behind can wash some hair and cook some food! And besides, he takes really good care of me." Wiggling on the stool, I start my mental search for proof to back up the last compliment. As the bartender placed the hot calamari between our wine glasses, I overwhelm my mouth with the spicy crunchy dish. Jasmine stared blankly at me. "He loves God, loves his family, and is extremely successful. In that sense, he reminds me of my father, and you know—"

"...*my daddy is such a good daddy*! Yes, Ken, we all know. Papa Johnson is the bomb, but you don't screw your daddy, Kendall!" Jasmine blurted, breaking her stare to fill her saucer with calamari.

I rolled my eyes and took another sip of wine to calm my nerves. As always, she was sarcastically right on point. James had a lot of great traits, but the passion and connection were lacking. The fact that I preferred spending time with Kenton than with him was a problem.

"Let me ask you this, Kendall." Jasmine shifted on her stool, clutching my hand with her left hand and grabbing the empty glass in her right. "Do you miss him when he's away? When you dream about your future ambitions, is he included? Do you smile to yourself when you think about him? Do you brag about him to your family and friends? When talking to God, do you innately pray for his well-being? Is he an asset or a liability? Can you imagine putting up with his crap for the rest of your life and still be satisfied? Do you at least enjoy kissing him, because we already know his schlong ain't stroking *shit*? Do you—"

"Wait, wait, wait! What? Enough with the interrogation, Judge Judy, my gosh! What's your point?" snatching my hand away to accentuate my irritation.

Jasmine giggled as she sensually waved her empty glass in the air, signaling the waiter for more. "I need you to go and get clinically tested for ADD, because clearly you can't focus. What I'm basically asking, is do you love him? Kendall Marie, do you love Dr. James "Dick Fingers" Smith?"

We immediately burst into laughter.

"Dr. Dick Fingers! Huh? Really? I'm afraid to even inquire about this nickname."

"Well, think about it, Ken, was it his fingers in your hair or his penis between your thighs that gave you an orgasm? It definitely wasn't both!"

"Oh wow. See, that is exactly why I don't tell you anything! Real relationships are about more than sex, Jasmine! He is good to me. Clearly you don't—"

Before my words could lash out and follow my frustration into a moment of regret, an angel of grace halted our evolving argument.

"Hey, sexy chicks!"

We turned around to find Carrie sashaying toward us, with her bronze-stained lips and dimpled smile. Her slim, curvaceous frame added a drumming beat to compliment the piano notes floating throughout the lounge. Still slightly pigeon-toed, her attempts to correct it resulted in more sway in her hips. After kissing us both on the cheek, she pulled a stool from the table behind us and intentionally nestled herself between Jasmine and me.

"Hey y'all! So, what's tonight's scandalous topic of conversation?"

Eager to make myself the victim, I sarcastically respond, "Jasmine, as always, is hating on my relationship with James. Oh, I'm sorry, Dr. Dick Fingers!" After taking another sip of my Merlot, this time leaving nothing behind, I asked the bartender for another glass. I couldn't tell if I was enjoying the wine or trying to bury the truth.

"Hmm! So, Jasmine told ya about our nickname for him, huh? Interesting!" Carrie curtly cut her eyes at Jasmine before grabbing my hands. "Well, sis, ya settling honey. And honestly, I feel like ya doin' this because ya don't wanna be alone. But, it's better to be single and alone than married and lonely."

Ouch, that hurt. Before the waiter could even place my glass on the counter, I grabbed it from him and took another long gulp. Lost in thought, I started circling the tip of my index finger around the rim of the Bordeaux wine glass. "Carrie, I wouldn't expect you to understand. You have always been in perfect relationships and ended up marrying the perfect guy. And, Jasmine, you... Aww heck, you are like the modern day video vixen..."

"Excuse me! Don't label me just because I don't give it up for free boo. Besides, sex is my preferred expression of spirituality. When I intimately connect with another man or even woman, without words, just pure sexual energy..." she paused briefly, inhaling deeply as she reminisced about her most recent experience, "...that's orgasmically elevating for me. And I would like to stress that I'm choosing to experience these moments. It's *not* out of obligation or fear of loneliness. My conscious decisions only expand my freedom as a living being. That's true spirituality to me." Jasmine preached.

Sexually, Jasmine identified herself as heterosexual, despite occasionally engaging in erotic encounters with women. When questioned about her lesbian tendencies, she said the connection with her female lovers served to balance out her need for emotional reciprocation from men, reducing the risk of her becoming too attached and needy. Although I completely disagreed with her logic, my love for my friend suppressed my innate desire to judge. If anything, I secretly envied her courage to embrace all of who she was, even if it made others uncomfortable. Besides, I had to contend with my own issues.

"I'm sorry. I hope you know I'm playing with you, Jas. Blame it on the alcohol!" I smiled at Jasmine and blew her a kiss of truce. She accepted by blowing me a kiss back. "Honestly, my answer to the parade of questions you just asked would be a unanimous *no*. I definitely don't love James. Actually, I think he's planning to propose to me soon, and that terrifies me."

"Are ya serious?" Carrie exclaimed. "What makes ya say that?"

Sulking deeper into my stool, I release a long exhale. "He wanted us to go to a local wine vineyard tomorrow for a weekend getaway. Out of fear that he might use this as an opportunity to propose, I lied and told him I promised my brother I would drive him back to college this weekend. You all know Kenton and I cannot be around each other for more than an hour without arguing."

"Exactly! That's what Jas and I are talking about, Kendall! Why subject ya'self to this? Now, Mile's crazy behind isn't perfect. He's my perfect, though! We've been married for almost a year, and sometimes I just wanna strangle him. But ya know he's my best friend. Even now, I'm missing my bookie. I couldn't imagine feeling the way ya do right now and ya not even married!"

"Well, what am I supposed to do? I'm terrified of being alone. Scared that if I throw away our two years I risk never having another chance with someone else. At twenty-seven, I kind of prefer to take the chance on him. I mean, what am I supposed to do?" I cried out, focusing my eyes on the flickering candle in the center of our table to calm my growing anxiety.

"Leave him!" Jasmine and Carrie shouted in unison, followed up with a high five of acknowledgement.

"Of course, you would say that. If only it were that easy." I swallowed the last sip of my wine, gathered my purse, and kissed my girls on the cheek. My heart and head had endured enough truth for one night.

It's better to be single and alone, than married and lonely. Trade in settling for patience.

Embrace ALL of who you are, even if it makes others uncomfortable. Own You!

Seven

"He did what?" I roared, propping my hands on my hips. "Calm down, Kendall Marie! Like I said, he stopped by to say hello and to drop off a gift for the family. Don't act so stunned. This theatrical display is not necessary. Besides, you terminated the relationship with him, remember? If you weren't so mesmerized by status, you would be meeting him at the altar instead."

He was the only guy I ever loved, but abandoned, instead choosing my guilt and fear. Although not the primary cause, there was a shallower reason for breaking up with him. At that time, Carvin lacked the good looks that I had listed on my "What I Look for in a Husband" list. Yes, I was attracted to fine men, with big bucks and status. That's why I held on so tightly to James. He was a prestigious doctor, with looks to match and a body chiseled like an African warrior. In contrast, the Carvin I fell in love with in college ran from the gym. He swore basketball shorts, a white T, and Converse were fashionably correct for all occasions. Although he was extremely intelligent, his lack of true vision and goals beyond graduate school left me uneasy about his ability to provide. Yet, I still loved him.

"So, what did he say? It's been like three years since we even spoke, so I'm just surprised he had the nerve to stop by."

Mom grabbed the pitcher of her famous homemade lemonade from the kitchen and placed it on the coffee table.

After pouring me a glass, she smoothed her signature khaki capris before sitting next to me on the living room couch. As usual, she took her sweet, southern time.

With my patience losing patience, I waved my hands in front of her as she slowly placed her feet on the ottoman. "Mom, please! Enough with the suspense."

"Calm down, Kendall Marie. You already know I don't rush for no one but Jesus. Now, let me get comfortable." Mom leaned back in the couch and took a sip of her drink. "Like always, he was very pleasant. He appears to be doing well and his business is flourishing. No longer fat, just slightly hefty. Actually, he's quite toned. Still not the best dressed, but he looks really, really good. He did ask about you—"

"What did he say?" I blurted, biting my bottom lip as I refused to allow my last breath to escape.

"Breathe, child! If you give me a moment, I will tell you. He asked how you were doing, if you were married, and if you were happy. I told him you were enjoying the work you were doing as a photojournalist and that you were, for the most part, happy."

"What about the other question, about marriage? Did you tell him I was engaged?"

"Oh, yeah, that. Yes, I told him you are unhappily engaged to a man you don't love."

"Mother!"

Mom winked at me as she flashed her gapped smile. "Of course not, sweetheart! But I did tell him you are engaged. He seemed genuinely happy for you. More happy for you than you are for yourself."

Mom was so right about that! As luck would have it, James did propose to me, and I reluctantly said yes. I thought if I steered away from any romantic dates, weekend getaways, or family gatherings with him, I could postpone what I knew was lurking around the corner. Except, James asked me when I least expected it, while he was washing my hair. When he asked, I was so engrossed in ecstasy that I shouted out *yes*. When I realized what had happened, it was too late. He was celebrating around the kitchen doing his Kappa stroll, and I was too much of a coward to take back my *yes*.

"Kendall Marie, when I met your father, he looked like a praying mantis. Tall and lanky, with a head that wasn't proportionate to his body. Oh, and he had these bifocal glasses and an asymmetrical haircut." Mom laughed out loud as she reminisced about the beginning stages of her lifetime love affair.. "He just looked a hot mess. For months, he was relentless at trying to capture my attention, but like you, I was being superficial. Overtime, I got to know him and realized how much fun we had together. Not only that, but he made me feel things, things that I had never felt before with any other man." She smiled to herself before taking a bite of her freshly baked raisin bread. "As I allowed myself to open up, I saw his potential and the gifts that were hidden within. Before long, I was in love and didn't care what others thought. Now I look at him and think, what if I had followed what I wanted instead of what I needed? Your father is truly the best thing that ever happened to me!"

"Aww, how sweet, Mom. But a praying mantis? That's harsh." I couldn't help but laugh at her dramatic story telling.

"Now hold on, Kendall! What you see now is a result of all my sweet lovin', good cooking, prayers, and respect for your father and his dreams. As the Bible boldly professes, 'He who finds a wife finds a good thing *and* obtains favor from the Lord.' When your father found me, he found his favor. Don't get it twisted, Miss Kendall Marie, your daddy is sprung!" Mom snapped her fingers in a Z-formation and smiled that dreamy-eyed smile that only thoughts of Dad could arouse.

"Oh goodness! Here you go." I chuckled. "James and I can have the same thing, right?" I looked at Mom with eyes begging for confirmation. I needed validation that with marriage I would learn to love him and God's favor would transform him into the man I wanted.

"Baby, that's for you to seek God about." Mom leaned over and filled our glasses with more lemonade. "The difference that I see with me and your father is that I was completely in love and satisfied with the man that he was before we got married. And his idiosyncrasies, I had already accepted them. I didn't marry him with the expectation that God would transform him into my knight in shining armor. He had earned that title before we even said 'I do'. You can't date or marry someone with the hope that they will change. If that's the case, you might need to change your mind about marrying James. Believe me, marriage will only magnify what issues you already have."

As tears began to stream down my face, Mom pulled me closer and laid my head on her lap. As she gently brushed my hair from my face and patted my shoulder, the internal battle thundered within me. With James, I knew financial security was guaranteed. What kept me going was the hope that my love for him would come after our nuptials.

Between sobs, I asked Mom one more question. "Do you think Carvin still loves me?"

Mom was silent for a moment. I could sense her smiling to herself. "Kendall Marie, I don't think anything. I *know* he still loves you. He's a wonderful young man, with an amazing heart and a bright future. I guess that's why he still has your heart, isn't it?"

"I guess so," was all I could muster the strength to say as images of Carvin danced between my feelings of fear and regret.

"Kendall, chasing perfection is like chasing the wind. Believe it or not, there is no such thing as the perfect man or woman. Don't pray for the answer, because that will come if it hasn't already, but pray that you have the courage and strength to be obedient to God's direction. Sometimes, I believe the hardest part is not hearing from God, but being obedient to His voice." Mom reached over me and grabbed a yellow fleece blanket out of the oak wood chest. She laid it over me and embraced me tighter. "Now close your eyes, honey, and rest your little heart."

Mom continued to comfort me with her gentle touch and loving spirit, as I prayed for courage to find me and allowed sleep to release me from my pain.

A few hours later, I woke up to silence as the setting sun waved through the bay window. Slowly raising my headache-stricken head, I rubbed my heavy eyes and reached for the glass of lemonade and two Tylenols left by Mom. As I placed the empty glass back down, my attention landed on a note from Mom and a sealed envelope. It simply read:

When you think about your life fifty years from today, ponder over what actions you will regret most and run from them! Run toward what will bring you lasting fulfillment, even if it doesn't make sense in the present. As you pray to God, ask Him for the courage to truly forgive yourself, accept the love you deserve, and be obedient. He will NEVER steer you wrong.

Love,
Mom

My eyes slowly traced over her letter a couple more times, allowing the words to comfort my distress. After placing her note to the side, I tore open the envelope and was amazed by the words that danced across the paper.

Hi, Ken,

I stopped by to see your parents, secretly hoping I would run into you. Your mom told me you're chasing your dreams, and that you had caught one—a husband. I'm happy for you. Thank you for always pushing me to be and do more. Recently, I moved to Houston and I'm living my dream right now. Thank you for always being my source of inspiration. God bless you, Ken.

Carvin

My heartbeat sped up, almost skipping over itself. As I read Carvin's words, repeatedly, my soul devoured each syllable and my desire for him intensified. While reading it for the seventh time, the garage door closing startled me, as James strolled into the living room.

"Hey, baby, what are you reading that has you glowing like a supernova?"

Shocked, I scramble to fold up the letter and stuff it back in the envelope, as he sat right next to me. To avoid discussing its contents, I asked what he was doing at my parents' house. "Hey, when did you get here? I didn't realize you were coming over. Where are my parents?"

"Your mom ran to the store and your dad is outside mowing the lawn. I stopped by because I couldn't reach you by phone. When you didn't come home last night, I was worried. I knew you would probably be at your parents', so I called your mom and she told me you were here. Why? Is it a problem for me to come over to my future in-laws house?" Before I could respond, James added, "And we need to work out this phone situation. Baby, I don't have time to chase you around all the time. This could all be resolved if you would just answer your phone when I call, or at least have the decency to text me back and let me know you're okay."

"Yeah, you're right." I nonchalantly agreed in hopes of moving the conversation to the next subject.

"Of course, I know I'm right. You're always saying I'm right, but not acting like it! That's really starting to irk me. I feel like you're blowing me lip service and I don't have time for that either. So, from now on I need you to be responsive when I call, understood?"

"No…" I curtly responded as I struggled to push myself up, holding on to the arm of the couch for support. Astonished by my honest response, I stopped mid-sentence. Clearly, James was, too.

"Good. Wait, what?" he fumbled.

I coughed nervously, trying to break up the growing knot in my throat. "No. I'm not going to be responsive when you call because I don't want to marry you. James, you're an awesome man, but I won't love you the way you deserve to be loved."

I stared down at James as he reclined back on the couch to get a better look into my eyes. "You're right. I'm a damn good man. But, what in the hell are you talking about? Come again!"

I heard God, as I had heard Him over the last year, but for the first time I was finding the courage to be obedient. It hurt tremendously, but I knew if I could find enough strength to push through this moment, I would avoid a lifetime of regret.

"I, um, I kinda feel like we need to hold off on the wedding. You're too good for me, and I—"

"Enough with the euphemisms! I need you to be direct. Just say it!"

"I don't want to marry you because I don't love you. I'm so sorry James."

James stared at me in silence, waiting for me to renege on my confession, but his silence was only met by mine. "Okay, so it took you two years to say this to me? Why in the hell did you agree to the marriage if you knew you didn't love me? I don't understand. Why would you introduce me to your family and friends, damn near move in with me, and waste my time, if you knew you didn't love me?"

Before I could open my mouth to respond, James stole the opportunity from me.

"Wait, don't even answer. Those were rhetorical questions because I already know the answer. You're desperate and lonely, and you thought I would be your golden ticket. You see, I've always known how desperate you are, I could smell it. I'm glad to know you've finally seen the light and mustered up the courage to be true to yourself. I love you, but I can get another chick with the quickness. I have options, and I'll be damned if I allow you to play games with me further."

I could see the tears welling in his eyes as he stared at me and then looked away. Putting his shades on to mask his heart break, he stood up, gathered his keys, and walked confidently to the front door.

As swiftly as he opened the door, James quickly closed it, turned around, and barged back toward me. He got within centimeters from my face, so close I could feel the heat of his anger slapping me. For a second I thought he was going to hit me. James grabbed my hand and calmly said, "Kendall, I am going to ask you this because I do love you and realize you can be impulsively stupid at times. Are you sure this is what you want? Are you sure you want to let all of me go? I want you to understand, you're risking never finding true love again. At twenty-seven, I'm not sure if you want to take that type of risk." Still gripping my hand, he stepped back, as if to give me a full view of his total package.

The fear of loneliness swept over me. The possible truth of his words left me feeling sick to my stomach and scared. Afraid that I had made a mistake, I wanted so desperately to blurt out, *"James, I'm so sorry! Please don't go. I just need time to think. I'm confused, please don't leave me alone,"* but the thought of an unhappy future, married to a man I don't love, stole my voice. I reached for whatever courage I could find and decided for once to bet on myself and God's promises.

"I can't, James. I realize you'll hate me, if you don't already, but you would detest me even more if I brought this into our marriage. You deserve to be with someone who will love the man you are… I'm sorry, but, I um, I'm just not her. I'm so sorry!" I collapsed back on the couch, exhausted from walking the plank of faith.

James stared at me with a look of disgust, pain, and love. He bent over and kissed me on the cheek. "As you wish. And please, don't call me once you realize you've lost the best thing you ever had. Don't you dare call me, Kendall!"

With that, he turned around and left, slamming the garage door behind him.

After I could no longer hear the engine of his Porsche revving down the street, I lay back on the couch and cried myself to sleep. Although some of my tears were from a place of sadness, the greater portion streamed from a place of gratitude. I was thankful that God had provided me with the courage that I needed to be obedient and follow His direction. Even in a moment of weakness, after I started taking those steps of courage, He never let me go. In that moment, as I drifted off to sleep, I heard my mother's words, *Now close your eyes, honey, and rest your little heart.* For the first time in two years, I was able to do just that.

 When seeking direction from God, also pray for the courage to be obedient to His voice.

Don't marry or date someone with the expectation that God is going to transform them into who you want them to be.

Being courageous doesn't indicate the absence of fear, but the will to ACT, despite its looming presence.

Bet on YOU! You're worth the risk.

Life Lesson

Eight

"You did what!"

"You broke up with Dr. Dick Fingers?"

After taking a couple weeks to digest the emotional freedom my courage afforded me, I decided to conference call Jasmine and Carrie to share the juice.

Jas seemed to be the most amused by my break up. "Hold up, let me look outside real quick." I heard rustling, probably Jas putting down the phone to look out her living room window.

"Ken, did Jas really just put down the phone? Anywho, while she is doing whateva it is she is doing, I need ya to explain what happened. As ya Matron of Honor, I went to Couture Bridal last night for my fitting and—"

Already anticipating what Carrie was going to say, I rolled my eyes and quickly interjected. I love my friend, but she has an exhausting habit of turning what only required a few words into a dissertation. "Sorry, Carrie, I will reimburse any costs you incurred. I wanted to tell you earlier, I just didn't know how."

Before Carrie could respond, Jasmine's voice burst into the receiver, breathing rapidly into the phone like she had just completed a marathon. "Whew! Sorry for jumping off the phone. I ran outside to look toward Heaven for a chariot of fire. Girl, I thought the second coming of Jesus was here!"

Just like Jasmine to dramatize her response. "Really? You act like my leaving James is a shock."

In unison, my friends chimed, "It is!"

"Since Jesus isn't on His way, what motivated you to finally follow the promptings of your heart? Carrie and I have been preaching to the choir for a while, I see we finally got an *Amen.*"

Without hesitation, I softly whispered through a slight grin. "God and Carvin." Since breaking up with James, my heartbeat grew louder for Carvin. All efforts to quiet my thoughts of him were futile. I dreamt about him when I slept and day dreamed about him while awake.

"*The* Mr. Carvin Alexander," Carrie chimed, putting emphasis on his name. "Wow, interesting. Please, please spill the soup."

For the next hour, I saturated their ears with details of my break up, the letter from Carvin, our recent meet up for happy hour, and our exercise date later today at Memorial Park. As much as I tried to suppress my smile and love for Carvin, I couldn't. Jas and Carrie picked up on my revived adoration, planning the next twenty years of our life without my consent.

"Ya know what, the couple down the street from me just put their townhome up for sale. Miles and I would love if Carvin and ya moved in. We can have date nights during the week and barbeques on the weekend." Before I could reel Carrie in from her fairytale, I heard her yelling for her husband as she attempted to cover the phone. "Hey Bae, ya won't believe who reunited and might be moving down the street!"

While Carrie carried on a side conversation with Miles, I attempted to convince Jasmine that I wanted nothing more than a friendship with Carvin. My efforts proved futile.

"Whatever, Kendall! You already know all attempts to hoodwink me are a waste of your breath and my time. I'm with Carrie—"

"Tell her, Jas," Carrie interrupted and then continued her side discussion with Miles.

"We know you love Carvin's streaked draws. Just let me know the date and time for the wedding. And, please, please make sure Carvin has some fine, successful brothas as his groomsmen. He was known for not having the cutest friends. I need a baby and a suga daddy fast! My flat stomach and robust derriere won't always be my allies."

"Will do," is all I could say as I tried to recapture my breath between laughter.

"But, seriously, we're so happy for ya, sis," Carrie interrupted. "Ya deserve a man whose love takes ya breath away. God wouldn't have it any otha way. Although at times we impatiently settle for the *any otha way.*"

"Awww, thanks, Carrie!"

"Oh, that was a fly line, Carrie. *A love that takes your breath away* sounds so poetic. On that note, cheers to you choking on Carvin's love, girl!" Jas chimed, as we all laughed.

Once we recovered from Jas's last comment, we spoke for a couple more minutes and shared a few parting words before hanging up. After tossing my cell phone in my gym bag, I stared at my reflection in the wall length mirror next to my fireplace. Dressed in my favorite electric blue leggings, pink Nikes, and yellow sports bra, I smiled at my well-kept frame.

Excited about the possibility of a possibility with Carvin, I grabbed my pink and green gym bag and rushed out the door, praying this workout would last a lifetime.

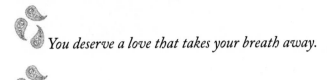

True friends will help you navigate through your hard times and celebrate during your happy times.

You deserve a love that takes your breath away.

In all aspects of your life, don't settle for the "any other way," only accept God's way, which is the best way.

Life Lesson

Nine

There is nothing more depressing than being educated and talented, with a bank account that's broke and almost non-existent. If I had known my degree would cost more than my salary, I might have pursued a trade with a greater return on my investment. I love photography as much as I love writing, which was why I chose to chase my dream of becoming a photojournalist. With James gone, I was really feeling the reality of my financial drought. Living paycheck to paycheck had me ready to trade my camera in for a stethoscope or a gavel. I had even flirted with the idea of a stripper pole, but my good girl conscious wouldn't let me twerk for cash.

My love for photography developed the summer before I started sixth grade. At least twice a month, Dad and I would go fishing in Galveston and binge on peanuts. During these times, he would humor me with his funny childhood stories or enlighten me about the Civil Rights era. One Sunday afternoon, we hiked back to the car with our fishing supplies, bragging among ourselves about our several catches of the day. The sun, as if seeking revenge for the lives we hooked from the ocean, tried relentlessly to burn our golden skin and suffocate us with its humidity. Eager for relief, we sought refuge under the shade of a welcoming willow tree. While we rested, Dad opened his knapsack and took out a Ziploc bag full of pictures and old newspaper clippings.

"Wow, what are all these?"

"Open it and see," Dad said, with a huge smile decorating his face.

"I don't get it. Who are these people? Wait, is this Dr. Martin Luther King, Jr.? And, is that you next to him?" I looked up at Dad wide-eyed.

"That sure is! As a matter of fact, these pictures were captured with my camera. I'm honored to say that your daddy was the fortunate eye behind the lens. After saving up all of my allowance, I brought a used Kodak Motormatic 35F Camera. I used it for the first time during a rally that Dr. King held at my local church."

"What about these, you took them, too?"

"Come on now, of course I did! My church Pastor was so impressed with my photos that he sent them to one of our local newspapers and voila! Several of the pictures were published."

For the next hour, Dad went through several pictures, illustrating the most fascinating story of his 1967 encounter with Dr. Martin Luther King, Jr. My love affair with photography began that day.

That following Christmas, my parents surprised me with my first camera, a KODAK STAR Zoom 105. From then on, I became the personal Johnson Family photographer.

By the time I made it to high school, I started challenging myself to tell stories without the use of words, but through a montage of photos. During my senior year, for my Persuasive writing term paper, I documented poverty in my city and captured it through photography. That alone was enough to persuade my classmates to organize a school wide service project, collecting food and clothes for local homeless shelters.

After graduating college, I spent several years entertaining temporary projects to build my portfolio and strengthen my craft. I landed odd jobs here and there, but never anything sustaining. In an effort to trade in Top Ramen for filet mignon, I applied for a position as a full-time Lead Photojournalist at a local newspaper. I had been deliberately preparing for this position. By accepting temporary assignments at this company, I hoped to better position myself to network and build my resume.

My efforts were slowly starting to pay off. I accepted a part-time Associate Photojournalist position. During this time, I befriended the Senior Secretary and would often find myself consulting her for spiritual counsel. Mrs. Zaldana originally migrated to the United States from Guatemala, in search of better opportunities for her and her four children. After marrying a prominent pastor in the Hispanic community, she often used her platform to advocate for the social rights of immigrants. Along with her passion for justice and insane work ethic, she held a deep reverence for God that I admired. Despite her broken English, she shared spiritual insight that often left me dumbfounded, and always gave me strength.

One evening in particular, as I rushed to my cubicle after fighting the torrential rain abusing Houston, Mrs. Zaldana intercepted my mad dash and asked that I visit with her before she left for the day. As I patted dry my chiffon blouse and reapplied my favorite red lipstick, I allowed the floor heater under my desk to revive my numb toes. Once presentable, I walked a few feet over to Mrs. Zaldana's desk and sat down in the chair facing her. She proceeded to whisper that a position had just opened for a Lead Photojournalist and urged me to apply. My eyes grew big and my smile spread wide over the possibility of being hired on full-time. Yet, as soon as the joy set in, the fear quickly followed.

"Oh Dios mios! Kendall, you doubt, pero que? You work hard. Senora Andy Williams would be muy loca not to hire you!"

"Awww, thank you, Mrs. Zaldana! I swear, you believe in me more than I believe in myself. I'm really not all that, as much as I may fake it! I'm talented, but so are the hundreds of other candidates that are applying. Competition is steep! I want it so bad, but I don't want—"

"My dear, save tu confessiones por Jesus! La job es yours mi amor. You are the child *of the Most High God.* What you receive es no because of you, pero His Grace. Mi confidence in what I say es porque no of who you are, pero mi Dio. Do you understand He can move competition?" Mrs. Zaldana stood up from behind her desk and took a seat on the edge, right in front of me as she placed my trembling hands between hers. "Take un second step, apply por la job and watch God. Exercise tu faith!"

"Yeah, you're right. It's just, I really don't want to get my hopes up just yet, though. I don't want to claim it if it's not what God has in store for me. I know I could bring so much talent to this position. If it's meant to be, God—"

"Again, mi nina, save tu confessions por Jesus." She pulled me forward and gave me one of her Big Momma hugs as she whispered in my ear, "Es yours senorita!"

As Mrs. Zaldana gathered her personal items to head home for the day, I sat in the chair opposite her desk, allowing her words and my doubts to battle like beta fish in the bowl of my mind. *Am I really ready? Would God honor my efforts and give me the desires of my heart? His word says delight yourself in the Lord and He shall give you the desires of your heart. I delight myself in Him, don't I? Can I do the job? But, God can do exceedingly and abundantly above all that I could ever ask, think or imagine. What if I fail? What if...* My thoughts were interrupted as Mrs. Zaldana reminded me to trust God and put my faith into action before hugging me goodbye.

I hurried back to my cubicle, grabbed my laptop, and spent the rest of the evening updating my resume and completing the application. I said a prayer, pleading for God to honor my wavering faith; hoping Mrs. Zaldana's faith was enough for the both of us. After two deep breaths, I mustered up all my faith, and pressed *submit*.

As luck would have it, I was selected for an interview and made it to the final round. Due to the positive response from my initial interviews, I was confident that this final one would be a breeze. It was apparent the interviewers were highly impressed with my portfolio and initiative in my current role. After a couple of weeks of biting my nails and jumping every time my cell phone chimed, the call I had been impatiently waiting for arrived. Unfortunately, the apologetic voice of the Human Resources Representative stated that the position had been offered to my competitor. I was crushed.

When I told Mrs. Zaldana, her response was a stark contrast to my deflated faith. "Senorita Kendall, what you think es un period es una comma in your story? Just wait, mi Dios ways are higher than yours y His thoughts are mas grande than yours. Bloom where you are planted and have faith. All will work out por tu good mami. In the end Jesus always wins." As hard as it was, I traded in my anger for her wisdom.

A year went by and I continued to *bloom where I was planted*. I took on more assignments and continued to apply for external positions. One day in particular, as I sat in my cubicle writing up an article for my recent photo exposé, I was startled when Ms. Andy Williams asked me to stop by her office. Thoughts of worst case scenarios invaded my mind. After months of grinding and trying to prove why I should have been selected for the lead position, the idea of being fired or laid off suspended my breathing. I rushed over to Mrs. Saldana's desk and whispered, "Pray for me," as I nodded toward Andy Williams's door.

Her smiling lips mouthed "God's got you" while pointing to Heaven.

With the sweat of anxiety starting to trickle down my forehead, I took a quick detour to the restroom to straighten my suit, dry my underarms, and pray for God's grace to go before me. I gently knocked on Ms. Andy Williams's door. Once she gave permission, I entered.

"Hi, Ms. Williams. You asked me to stop by your office?"

"Yes, Kendall, please call me Andy. Don't be so nervous, take a seat."

"Oh, okay, thanks." I timidly scooted around the zebra print wing chair and took a seat.

"I wanted to talk to you about your performance and career path. For the record, you were one of the top candidates for the Lead position. When you weren't selected, I forewarned your supervisor that we would probably lose you to our competitor. When I saw that you not only stayed, but your work ethic improved, I was highly impressed. In this field, I've learned to measure someone's character by how they respond to disappointment." She smiled to herself, as if satisfied by her own profoundness.

"Honestly, I don't know what to say. Let me start with, thank you." Feeling this encounter may not be as negative as I assumed, I slowly inched further back into the chair and allowed my arms to relax.

"No, I need to thank you for elevating the morale of your team and consistently producing insightful, dynamic work." Ms. Andy Williams stood up and walked over to her mini refrigerator. It's amazing to see a woman with such a masculine name bear such a feminine frame. She was absolutely beautiful, and to my surprise, very pleasant. She poured herself a glass of scotch and sat back down. I dared not question her violating the Zero Tolerance Policy for alcoholic beverages at work. Instead, I continued to admire her beauty and smile.

"I would like to hire you on full-time as a Senior Lead Photojournalist. I'm not sure if this has hit the rumor mill yet, but Marcus has accepted a position with the *New York Times*, so he will be resigning as the Senior Lead. When I asked him and your supervisor about a potential successor, your name was recited by both. I value their opinion, but more importantly, I trust my intuition."

I almost fell out of my seat. *Me, as a Senior Lead, really?* This superseded what I envisioned for myself. I was just hoping to one day be hired on as a full time Lead. Andy opened up the top drawer of her mahogany desk and pulled out a white envelope. "Please review this job description and salary offer. Our Human Resources Director will be in touch with you tomorrow to extend a formal offer."

"What about the interview, will there be an interview?"

Andy smiled. "Actually, an interview is not necessary. Without knowing it, I've been interviewing you over the past year by observation. You passed!"

"Ms. Andy Williams, I am—"

"Please, call me Andy."

"I'm so sorry. Andy, I'm speechless. Wow! Thank you. I will certainly review the job responsibilities, and wait to hear from the HR Director. My God, I'm overwhelmed with gratitude!"

Noticing myself bouncing in the wing chair with each word, I quickly composed myself, brushing my sweaty palms against my pin-striped pencil skirt.

Appearing overwhelmed by my recent recital of excitement, Andy closed her eyes and took another sip. "Thank yourself for consistently displaying integrity, diligence, and outstanding talent in your current role. You earned this, keep it up. Don't make me regret this moment." Andy swiveled in her chair to her computer and went back to work. Without looking up, she dismissed me with an abrupt, "Thank you for your time, Ms. Johnson. Please close my door behind you."

With that, I stood up, grabbed the envelope from her desk, and headed to the door.

Before leaving, I beamed back at her and extended my gratitude again. "Thank you so much, Andy."

Without removing her eyes from her computer she responded, "Please call me Ms. Williams. You're welcome, Ms. Johnson."

After closing her door, I started doing the funky chicken right outside. I was so excited and couldn't hide it. Finally, I was starting to see the fruits of my labor and they tasted delicious!

 A temporary delay is not a permanent denial.

 Bloom where you're planted.

The true measure of one's character is not in how they respond to joyful moments, but how they react during challenging times.

Life Lesson

Ten

I love him. I love him not. I love him. I love him not. I love him....

One thing I was more certain of, other than the unconditional love of my parents, was that I absolutely adored Carvin Alexander. When we initially embarked on this love journey, I didn't see nor appreciate the man he was destined to be. Which explained why, I rebounded into the arms of Dr. James "Dick Fingers" Smith. It's amazing what space and time could teach someone; it definitely taught me to love beyond my fears.

Despite what my eyes had previously shown me, Carvin matured into his handsome. To say he was fine would be an exaggeration. Unlike me, he wasn't the fashion connoisseur. Although he had traded in his basketball shorts, white T-shirts, and Converse for creased Khaki pants, a white Polo, and Sperrys, Carvin was still simple in appearance. Nothing more, nothing less. Now I, on the other hand, was a fashion addict. Rocking the hottest heels, trendiest clutches, and colorful dresses were my signature look. When out together, to the onlookers, we were like a walking Yin and Yang pendant.

Physically, he was constantly compared to Cedric the Entertainer, with the humor to match. Carvin always had a way of turning my frown into a smile, and my smile into tears of laughter. Tickling my funny bone was one of his greatest attributes and one of the many reasons why I fell in love with him. Along with him being a driven entrepreneur, family oriented, spiritual, respectful, and absolutely in love with all of me, he was my best friend.

Oh, and I can't forget to pay homage to his mind. His innate ability to express himself always inspired me to be more purposed with my words. I often found myself mesmerized by the knowledge that poured from his lips. We would get lost for hours in conversations about an array of topics. On any given night, you could find us lying by his fireplace with a glass of Merlot, cuddling as we journeyed from one topic to the next. Eventually, our discussions would evolve into a debate, and the passion behind our individual arguments would erupt into steamy lovemaking. Deliberately starting a random debate about a trivial topic, just so we could enjoy the sex afterward, was one of our favorite extracurricular activities!

Despite having a relatively strong friendship, we did encounter our hiccups. One of the deepest thorns in our relationship was our contrasting opinions about having children. We often debated about this subject, but unlike our other debates, it rarely ended with his lips between my thighs.

"So let me make sure my interpretation of your insanity is accurate. You don't want to have any children… Ever?"

"Carvin, we have been through this before. Why, oh why, do we continue revisiting this topic? Like I said during our last argument, N.O. spells no. I don't want children… Ever!"

We were driving through Mid-Town, just leaving a housewarming party for his best friend Terrell and his wife. They had just given birth to their first child, Sela, and had asked Carvin to be her godfather. Enchanted by Princess Sela, Carvin was taking every opportunity to hold her. As we hugged the host and hostess, and told the other guests "Goodnight," I gathered my strength, knowing that an argument would greet us on the ride back to his place.

Carvin continued to drive, looking over at me every so often, shaking his head.

"Enough is enough, Carvin. I refuse to allow you to treat me like I wear the scarlet letter! If you want a darn child so bad, go get a dog!"

"Really, Kendall! Really! You know I'm allergic to dogs, baby. You, of all people, should know after you damn near tried to kill me with one last year. I don't care what you say, I really think you were trying to murder ya boy!"

We burst into laughter as we reminisced about when I surprised him with a puppy bulldog, hoping it would subdue his paternal itch. Instead, he ended up in the emergency room and hospitalized for two days. Let's just say a family friend has since adopted Little Max.

"Whatever, Carvin! Now, if we were married and your life insurance policy was hefty, then you could get all conspiracy theorist on me. You're worth more alive than dead to me. At least for right now!" I winked and blew a kiss at him. Carvin caught my imaginary kiss, rolled down the driver's side window, and tossed it out.

"Look, Ken, I just can't wrap my mind around your adamancy against having children."

"Here we go again..." Flipping down the passenger's side mirror as I attempted to secure my loose tresses into a bun, I slowly crossed my eyes and let out a heavy exhale to further emphasize my annoyance with where the conversation was headed.

"Naw, but seriously! I'm a damn good man and more importantly, I love you. Oh, and we can't overlook how well I keep you fed. You kicked those Oscar Mayer weenies to the curb once you got a taste of Big Poppas kielbasa!" Again, we laughed as he started easing his hand up my skirt. As I embraced his hand and guided it deeper toward my love gem, he abruptly pulled away.

"Baby, don't stop." I leaned over and whispered in his ear. "I have a pantiless surprise for you."

Carvin yanked his head away from me, despite the growing bulge in his pants. "Kendall, I'm serious. Seeing you barefoot and pregnant in my kitchen would be kinda sexy." I grabbed my sequined clutch and smacked him on the arm as he laughed. Even in a serious moment, he can't help interjecting a joke to lighten the mood. But, given the gravity of this topic, I started to find his jokes irritating.

"Your chauvinism is *not* attractive. Honestly, I'm getting tired of talking about this. I can't explain it and I certainly don't expect you to understand, but I do ask that you respect my stance. I *do not* want children, Carvin. Period. Now, can we please stop talking about this while we're still amicable? I really don't feel like arguing tonight!"

"But why, Kendall? I think I deserve a reason why. Don't you?"

"Just because, okay?" Before Carvin could pry further, I turned up the music and closed my eyes. Fully aware of my selfishness, Guilt wouldn't allow me to be honest with him about my past. For the rest of the ride home, I sank into the passenger seat and allowed the camel colored leather to cradle me to sleep.

As we pulled up to his house, he parked outside of his garage and got out the car. He came around and opened the passenger side door to help me out. That's another trait I loved about him, he was always chivalrous, even when upset. As we walked toward his front door, Carvin took the opportunity to dampen the mood further.

"No, it's not enough, Kendall. I want the woman I love to carry my seed. I don't see what the problem is with that. You want all of me on your terms, and that ain't cool. I put up with your crap, doing all that I can to make you happy and you refuse to even consider doing the one thing that will bring me lasting joy. And, when I ask you why, your only reason for your selfishness is some half-assed 'just because'. What the f—."

Carvin avoided cursing around me, so right when he was about to release another expletive he abruptly quieted himself and pushed past me toward his porch. After opening the front door, he kissed me on the forehead and proceeded to walk back toward the car.

"Ummm, excuse me. Where are you going?"

He turned around, throwing his hands up in the air, "you have to be kidding me right now! If my memory serves me correctly, you said you didn't want to argue tonight. I, on the other hand, want to discuss this matter like the two grown adults we are. Since I *refuse* to talk to the wall and I certainly don't want to say something to you that I'll later regret, I think the best compromise is for me to go chill at my brother's place for the night. I'll be back in the morning."

With that, he got in his car and drove off, leaving no opportunity for my rebuttal.

Compromise is not intended to be one-sided.

In order to succeed in love, whether romantic or platonic, you must allow yourself to be vulnerable; find the courage to remove masks.

Eleven

One thing I tried not to do was allow my past to dictate my future, but in the case of childbearing, my past directed my every decision. Carvin and I continued to argue about my disdain with having children, but I couldn't bring myself to tell him the reason why I was cold to the idea. I preferred arguing any day over divulging the truth of my rape and the adoption. Although I no longer blamed myself for attracting Davis's offensive violation, the Guilt behind giving my son up for adoption only grew riper with time.

The first Friday of every month, Jasmine, Carrie, and I would meet at Wine-O Rita, our favorite wine and margarita bar, for happy hour and gossip. Carrie had recently announced that she and her husband were expecting, so she decided not to put herself in temptation's way, afraid the house margarita might find its way in her hands. Refusing to cancel our ritual, Jasmine and I decided to meet up after work. Besides, I needed her guidance with overcoming my most recent argument with Carvin.

"Girl, just tell him the truth. Carvin is such a cool dude, unlike the scrubs I tend to entertain. You really need to give him more credit, Kendall."

"It's not that easy, Jasmine. My stomach cringes at just the thought of telling him. Because his birth mom abandoned him, he is blatantly critical of women who turn to abortion or adoption."

"Okay, but you were *raped*. I think if he understood your reason for choosing to have your son adopted, he would consider that a selfless act. Right? When you found out you were pregnant, you could've had an abortion, but you chose to give your son life. I have so much respect for you, Kendall. That was not an easy thing for you to do. He would have to understand and love you even more for that! *Right?*"

"Clearly, you don't know my Carvin and his contempt for abortions and adoption. He feels all Planned Parenthoods need to be demolished. He is extremely conservative, darn near delusional, about it. He feels abortion is a crime of convenience and adoption is abandonment. And, to some extent, he's right about adoption. If I would have never given my son away, I might—"

Before Guilt could creep in, Jasmine called it out. "Not tonight! You are *not* going to pull up an extra seat and invite Guilt's trifling ass to crash our groove. I won't allow it, honey! Oh no, not tonight, boo." Jas shook her index finger to emphasize her point. "As for Carvin, has he considered counseling? I realize his parents aren't the greatest, but damn, I've never met perfect parents. Granted, at your Christmas dinner last year, I *was* a little perturbed when they started fighting at the table. Now, that was *real* ghetto."

Jas blinked repeatedly and chuckled as she relived that embarrassing event at my parents' house. Carvin was so humiliated. To this day, he still apologizes to my parents every time he sees them. But, she's right, it was definitely a Jerry Springer worthy performance.

"Yeah, that was crazy. My poor baby was mortified."

"Now that I think about it, you never divulged the juice about what they were throwing blows about. No better time than the present, spill it!" Jas leaned in closer, cradling her chin in her palms, as her goofy smile begged me to proceed.

"Utter ridiculousness! You remember my great aunt Britta who flew in from Chicago?"

"Yeah, your granny's older sister. How could I ever forget her? She cornered me on the way to the bathroom and forced me to listen to her story about the blowjob she gave her boyfriend. As much as I love talking about sex, having an eighty-five-year-old woman tell me about the blowjob she gave her younger boyfriend was not sexy at all!" Jas scrunched up her face, shaking her head as she tried to erase the image from her thoughts. "That shit was traumatic!"

"Hilarious! I totally forgot about that. Yep, that's Great Aunt Britta for you."

"So, what does she have to do with the boxing match between Carvin's parents?"

Given the absurdity of my response, I stared at Jasmine, debating if I should share this sweet gossip. As she wiggled in the booth, eyes twinkling with excitement, I leaned over the candle separating us and whispered it all., "Well, rumor has it she wanted to introduce Carvin's pops to her fellatio skills and he was actually down!"

Jas shot back in her seat, torso erect, and eyes wide. She started bouncing as she responded, "Girl, shut the hell up! No disrespect, but what would his dad see in Great Aunt Britta? She's old, can barely see, and toothless." Jas covered her mouth as if she had an epiphany. "Oh wait. Maybe that was his motivation. What man would refuse a gum job, huh?"

I almost spat out my drink as I fell over in laughter. "Jasmine, you're a fool! Actually, word on the street is that Carvin's dad has a fetish for elderly women. I guess that night Mama Alexander wasn't going to allow Great Aunt Britta to show her up. When she took off her wig and slung it across the table at him, I knew all hell was about to break loose!"

Waving her manicured hand in my face, Jasmine started snorting between her laughter as she proceeded to one up me. "Oh no, hunty, I have an even better one! The most outrageous part was when his mom took the pig's head off the dinner table and started chasing him around the kitchen with it. When she started shouting, 'You want some head! You want some head, you bastard! Bend over and take this head like the pig you are!' I was through! That was crazy-funny and sad! Utterly surreal!"

Jasmine and I shared a moment of silence as we digested all of the foolishness that took place on that horrid night.

"Awww, my poor Carvin. My baby was so pissed. And, that's another reason why I can't tell him the truth about why I don't want kids. Poor thing has enough dysfunction in his life."

"Whatever, Ken. That is *not* a sufficient excuse not to tell him. The real reason is fear and guilt. Let's get real, girl. You feel guilty about the adoption, which in turn has you afraid of how *he* will respond to *it*. To me, that's crazy because you have *nothing* to feel guilty about. But, guilt mixed with fear will make you do some crazy shit. I should know. In this case, he deserves to know and if he loves you, he will accept your past. But, hey, that's just my opinion. You do what you want to do." Jasmine grabbed her compact mirror from her purse and reapplied her ruby red lipstick, patting away the sweat highlighting her forehead.

A few moments of shared silence settled as her words lingered. "Yeah, you're right about the Guilt. It's like, I know what I need to do, but for some reason I can't will myself to do it. I just can't tell him. Ugh!" Not wanting tears to clump my mascara, I grabbed the wet napkin, catching the perspiration from Jasmine's melting margarita, and dabbed them away. "Let's just change the subject, please. I can't deal with this right now."

Jasmine gently grabbed my hand, staring at me through glossy eyes. "Are you sure you don't want to chat more? You know I'm all ears, girl." Nodding, I smiled for her to proceed. "Cool, I have a quick subject changer for you." Jasmine shimmied in her seat like a giddy schoolgirl.

"Ok, I'm listening." I leaned forward; somewhat relieved the topic was off me.

"So, my colleague, Shelly, convinced me to go with her to a Fraternity Gala last weekend. Everyone was adorned in suits and ties. I mean, these brothas were looking so delectable. And, you know your girl was looking sassy fly!" Jasmine sang as she put her right palm up and imitated looking in the mirror to admire her naturally curly afro, cinnamon bronzed complexion, and high cheekbones. "Anyhow, please tell me why the one chubby creep, with fro-dreads and ashy lips, had the *audacity* to approach me and ask for my number? He wasn't even in the fraternity, but was there helping with the sound system. Why in the hell do I get the same lame dudes approaching me? They say what you attract is a reflection of self. Am I lame and whack, Ken? Do I lack intellect, class, and a belt to hold up my oversized pants? Be honest, girl!"

As I gave Jasmine the once over, I was appalled that she would even make such an absurd inquiry. Jasmine stood an even six feet with light brown almond shaped eyes, Angelina Jolie lips, and a face kissed by freckles. My girl was fierce!

"Wow, Jasmine, are you seriously asking me this question right now? Granted, I said change the subject, but I didn't expect you to be so quick about it. I'm dealing with some serious emotional turmoil and you're asking me about some umpa lumpa Omega Psi Phi dude. Can we say selfish?"

"First, he wasn't an Omega and secondly *you* gave me permission to change the subject." Jasmine stared at me, perplexed. "Look, Ken, we visit the topic of you and Carvin every time we talk, for the majority of our conversation. What else can I say?

You need to tell Carvin the reason behind your shackled womb, that's the bottom line! You always preach about transparency and being *real*. I need you to get from behind the pulpit and live it!" Jasmine retorted matter-of-factly.

"I should have known you wouldn't understand. Forget about it." I reached for my clutch to grab my pressed-powder and wipe away my perspiring pity party. Jasmine was right, but I was feeling some type of way and arguing seemed like the best way to relieve my Guilt and displace my frustration with Carvin. Unfortunately, Jasmine was in aiming range.

"Okay, cool. Now, can I please get back on my dating life soap box?" Jasmine rolled her eyes.

I was astounded. Jasmine had been my sista-friend since sophomore year in high school and we never had an argument. She was always available to listen to my heartaches and help me sift through my drama. Granted, I was being a selfish brat, but Guilt had a way of making me feel like she needed to tolerate it. Looking back on it, I was being completely irrational.

"What is up with you, Jasmine?" I stabbed back. "Why are you acting like something I refuse to call you?"

Eyebrows hiked by my last comment, Jasmine twisted her neck as she peered at me with hurt and brewing anger. She leaned forward, tapping her index finger on the table to emphasize her point. "Are you insinuating I'm acting like a B.I.T.C.H? Ken, when was the last time you inquired about me, huh? When was the last time you asked about the forecast of my life? Let's see, it's been a long damn time. If you had, you would've known that I recently had a miscarriage and my grandma was diagnosed with cancer. Every single time we get together, you monopolize the conversation, talking about the same crap! We all go through shit, Ken. Instead of focusing so much on yours, dedicate some time helping others overcome theirs. You just might need to reevaluate who here is acting like a bitch!" As tears streamed down my friend's face, I felt my heart sink. As much as I wanted to be offended by her lashing out, the possible truth behind her words wouldn't allow me. Had I really been that disconnected and self-absorbed?

"Jasmine! Why didn't you tell me? We are sisters; you should never feel like you can't open up and tell me about what's going on in your life. I'm so sorry for being a B!"

By this time, Jasmine was using her hands as a tissue to wipe away the tears. I handed her a tissue of truce and she snatched it away. "Uh, hello! I've made multiple attempts. Whenever you ask how I'm doing, you always find a way to redirect the conversation back to you and that's where we linger. Lately, you've been so absorbed by all this guilt, it has you trippin'. You're my ace, so I love listening to your concerns and helping you resolve them. It's just sometimes it bothers me when you don't bestow the same courtesy. I'm sorry for lashing out at you, but I felt like that was the only way I could get your attention. I've been going through hell, Kendall. I need my friend to be my strength and listen to me for once. Can you please do that?"

Without hesitation, I went to the other side of the table and embraced my friend. We hugged as she allowed herself to cry in my arms. I took a seat right next to her and wiped her tears with a napkin. "Jasmine, I'm really sorry for not being there for you. You're one of my dearest friends and you've always been there for my craziness. I vow not to talk about myself for the next month. Starting right now!"

Not buying it, Jas rolled her eyes and laughed through sobs. "Heffa, please! You and I both know that is an impossible challenge for you. But, Lord knows I would love to see you struggle trying to live up to this promise. This is the best revenge a friend could ask for."

"Well it doesn't hurt to try. So, let's go back to my place and I'll pour you a glass of my new favorite Merlot. You can tell me all about your personal problems while I serve you some of my homemade chicken noodle soup. Wine and my chicken noodle soup, the perfect remedy for the soul!"

"And you won't talk about yourself?"

I paused for a moment, and then smiled. "I won't talk about myself. If I do, I'll call Carvin and tell him my deep, dark secret. Pinky promise."

Jasmine locked her freshly manicured pinky with mine.

"I think you have yourself a deal! Thanks, Kendall."

"Anytime. Okay, enough with the sappy. Let's go get tipsy off wine and chicken noodle soup."

"With a soda on the side!" Jasmine belted.

Two of the greatest gifts, outside of love, that you can give someone are to 1) ask "how are you doing?" and 2) listen compassionately when they respond.

Listen to the conversations you keep. Don't borrow the time of others complaining about the same thing and making no effort to bring about the change you desire. That's a poor use of your time and theirs.

Identify areas where fear and guilt are leading your life, and take back your power.

Life Lesson

Twelve

"I used to question God about when I would meet the perfect person, the woman that He fashioned to help bring life to my purpose. One day, my homeboy told me something so simple,. 'If every chick you met was the perfect one, you wouldn't recognize the right one when she appeared'. I kept those words close to my heart. And, when I met you I knew you were my perfect. Ken, I love everything about you. Even our differences, I can appreciate. You make me want to live and love beyond myself. To live my lifetime with you as my best friend, lover, confidant, and wife would bring me eternal gratitude. Would you grant me that honor? Kendall Marie Johnson, will you please, please, please marry me, baby?"

Life stopped. I forgot how to breathe, think, speak, or even be. I was lost in a whirlpool of emotions. Shock, excitement, fear, joy, confusion, and love rushed into every pore of my body. Surrounded by my family and friends for my thirtieth birthday celebration was paralyzing, as everyone peered at me awaiting a response that I didn't have. Adorned in a gold sequined cocktail dress, red stilettos, ringlet curls framing my face, and my signature cherry red lipstick, my freshly manicured hands trembled as he bejeweled my left hand with a beautiful princess cut diamond.

I knew that Carvin was my perfect. However, for the past few months I had doubted if I could be his. The culprit of my doubt was our conflicting beliefs on having children. The weight of the adoption had started to press down on my spirit, especially as our arguments about children became more frequent. Despite the feedback from my girlfriends, I shied away from telling him the truth about my past.

For my surprise birthday party, Carvin rented out a local Art Museum and adorned the walls with some of my greatest photography. I thought we were going to see the premiere work of Dom Kelvey, one of my favorite local photographers. I had no idea we would be going to an exhibit showcasing my work. I was floored! Even more impressive was having my family and friends, from near and far, join in the celebration.

The guests were dressed up in cocktail attire, grooving to the smooth ballads from the live band as they enjoyed delectable hors d'oeuvres and wine. The greatest gift was when Carvin auctioned off some of my artwork and announced the proceeds were going to my favorite non-profit that advocated community involvement and social justice: Sisters Advocating Second Steps, Inc. I was flooded with tears of gratitude, hugging my guests for being so generous with their donations. Although my six glasses of wine had a way of embellishing my emotions, I was sincerely touched to see my family and friends support my philanthropic interests. So, when Carvin called me to the front of the museum to present me with what should have been the epitome of my night, all present expected to see a similar display of emotion. Instead, they saw stoicism and heard silence. The silence was immediately shattered as my seventh glass of wine hit the marble floor.

"Kendall. Baby. Did you hear me?"

"Umm, yes. I, uh, I mean, I, uh…" As I looked around my eyes caught my mom beaming with joy, Carrie was mopping away her tears, and my dad was trying to hold back his. The rest of my family and friends either were in tears or giddy in anticipation of my saying *yes*. I looked back at Carvin as he knelt before me, staring through the eyes of gentleness and love I had grown to adore.

"Carvin, um, I need to tell you something. Babe, I'm not who you think I am. I did something in my past that I think you may find hard to forgive. Before I say *yes*, I need to tell you the truth."

Carvin, aware of my loose lips syndrome, tried to quiet me before I embarrassed myself in front of our guests. He looked around with hesitancy and then back at me, as he whispered, "Kendall, do you want to discuss this in private? I'm not sure this is the appropriate time for confession."

"Kendall, I think whatever you need to say can wait, don't you?" Jas hastily interjected, giving me an exaggerated, cockeyed look that pleaded for me to shut up.

Ignoring her pleas for my silence, I stuttered on. "Carvin, you don't want to marry me. You want children and I don't. I've always been scared to tell you why. Actually, I know you will leave me. Or, I think you will… I don't know. But I can't live like this anymore, especially if we plan to get married. I have—"

"Kendall Marie, stop, honey," Mom interrupted as she walked up and grabbed my hands. "This is not the time or the place. Your guests are here to celebrate your birthday and the man you love wants to marry you. Don't belittle this experience by having a come to Jesus moment." She then whispered in my ear, "Don't embarrass this amazing man who loves you and don't you dare embarrass yourself. Save your confessions for Jesus."

As Mom held my hands, we stared each other directly in the eyes. My racing thoughts disregarded her demands as Guilt prompted my words to spill forth.

"Carvin, when I was sixteen years old, I was raped by a classmate. As much as I detested that bastard for taking my innocence, he gave me a beautiful blessing, my son. Instead of raising my son, I gave him away. After I gave birth, I vowed never to have another child. To raise and love another child after I gave one away seems so selfish. I... I... I can't even imagine it."

Then, I let go of Mom's hands and turned to look at the man I loved. He stood in front of me, studying my eyes for an answer. "I never told you because I know how you feel about adoption. I was afraid that you would hate me and leave me. I was going to tell you as soon as I gathered the courage to accept your reaction. As much as I love you, Carvin, and want to say yes, I need you to understand that I'm rooted in my belief and have no intentions of changing my mind."

Carvin shook his head in disbelief, pacing back and forth. Our guests stood wide-eyed with mouths agape, waiting to hear his response.

"Wow, Kendall. So, you really decided to tell me this now. Right now!" his words stumbled out. "I'm so amazed by you. You always have a way of making a situation about you and messing up a perfect evening." He stood, and with his trembling hands, grabbed mine as he whispered, "Why didn't you tell me this sooner, Kendall?"

He let go of my hands, stepped back, and looked at me. I couldn't tell if he was looking at me with feelings of disgust or pity, but I was certain the look of adoration had disappeared.

Reaching for his hands, he snatched them away as he turned his attention to the floor. I turned to my guests, as tears streaked and smeared my makeup, and apologized for the turn of events. I gathered my purse and shawl and kissed my parents on the cheek as I rushed toward the front entrance. Secretly, I was hoping

Carvin would run after me, but when I turned around he was nowhere in sight. As I stepped outside into the cold, the winter chill pinched my cheeks, reminding me that what just happened was not a dream.

The one desire of TRUTH is to be told. When you choose not to speak your Truth, out of fear, you force Truth to present itself, sometimes at the most inopportune time. Honor your Truth by speaking it always, even when it hurts.

Life Lesson

Thirteen

Once home, attempts to rinse away my humiliation in a hot shower only managed to wash away my makeup. I must have sat on the porcelain floor for more than an hour, my tears competing with the beads of water as they raced toward the drain. Crawling out of the shower, I sprawled naked across my bed, allowing the ceiling fan to dry my drenched skin.

Lying motionless, memories of my first love invaded my thoughts. His smooth chocolate skin, gentle brown eyes, and thick black curls taunted me. Remembering our first kiss, and how he gazed at me with such innocence, prompted my tears. He was my first love and I was his. I could still smell his scent and hear his first wail as he greeted the world. Oftentimes, daydreams of my first love would emerge without permission, wondering where he lived, what he was like, how he looked, if he was happy, and if he knew how much I loved him. As I allowed visions of him to occupy my mind, I drifted off into a deep sleep.

Hours later, a kiss on the forehead startled me. My puffy eyes slowly opened to Carvin taking off his clothes, climbing into bed, and his naked body embracing me.

As soon as he kissed me on my shoulder, I felt myself slipping into a frenzy of tears.

"I'm so sorry Carvin. I don't know what I was thinking. I didn't expect you to come over tonight. I know you hate me and—"

"Shhhh." Carvin pulled me closer, laying his head against mine. "Kendall, I could never hate you. Baby, why didn't you tell me? How could you keep something so tragic from me? I could never judge you. What hurt's the most is that you would think so low of me. Why?"

"I don't know. I just... I just didn't have the courage to face the possibility of you leaving me. I still judge myself for my decision, so having the one man I love join me in my self-loathing was too much to fathom," I whispered between sobs.

Carvin turned my face to his and kissed my bottom lip. He sat up in the bed, beckoning me to follow his lead.

As I followed him from my bedroom, the darkness started to dissipate as we moved closer to the living room. I saw the dancing shadows of candles, painting the walls and the smooth sounds of KEM crooning in the background. When we turned the slight corner into my living room, a sea of candles and red rose petals greeted me. On the ledge of the fireplace was a bottle of my favorite Merlot and two empty glasses. As I turned to Carvin for an explanation, I was surprised to find him down on one knee, with a smile plastered across his face.

"Boy, what are you doing?"

"What I tried to do earlier today, ask the woman of my dreams to live a lifetime with me. Kendall, I get it, you don't want kids. For the first time I understand why. Lord knows I want kids, but I can't imagine my life without you. You're worth the sacrifice."

Bending down to search his piercing stare, I caressed the perimeter of his face with my fingertips. "But that's not fair to you. I love you too much to allow you to compromise your happiness for me."

"You are my happy, Kendall. It was so hard in the past for me to accept your view because you never told me the reason behind it. Tonight, despite it being at the *worst* time, you shared. I love you even more for that."

The growing knots in my stomach and swelling in my throat agitated my angst. Stepping back toward the fireplace, I grabbed the wine glass and brought it up to my parched lips only to realize its emptiness. Desperate to calm my racing thoughts, my clammy hands shook as I reached for the bottle and attempted to pour. Immediately, I felt Carvin's body heat competing with the crackling flames of the fire as he leaned against mine and reached for both my glass and the wine.

"Don't worry, baby, I got you," he whispered.

"You say that now, but how do you know you won't resent me later?"

Carvin tilted his head and furrowed his eyebrows. "Umm, for pouring you a glass of wine?"

"No, silly. For not giving you a child?"

"I know. I was just trying to lighten the mood." Carvin gently kissed me on the lips, parting my mouth with his tongue, and then replacing his lips with the rim of the glass. "Here, take a sip."

Succumbing to his gentle pour, I swallowed, allowing the sweet dryness to hydrate my nerves. "Carvin, how do you know?" I pleaded.

"Because I love you. I mean, there's always adoption. Wait, you're open to adopt, right?"

"I mean, I guess I could adopt, but I thought you were against the whole idea of adoption."

With a side grin, Carvin took a sip of wine, looking away as he shook his head. "Yeah, well, after you overdosed on truth serum and turned your birthday into a confession session, I realized my views were way too rigid. I recognize a lot of that has to do with my folks and issues I have with my birth mom. But the truth is I'm standing before you today because someone was selfless enough to adopt me."

He paused, as if in deep thought. "But, the thought of someone raping you enrages me." Flexing his fists, Carvin handed me the glass as he stepped away and crouched in front of the fireplace, scowling at the dancing flames as if they were taunting him. "As you headed to the door to leave, I couldn't stop thinking about you being raped. Honestly, I want to kill him right now!"

"He isn't worth it. I remember feeling that way, but I decided to forgive him a long time ago. It's me I need to forgive."

"So, why did you give your son up for adoption?" Carvin asked, still staring at the flames, but with less disdain.

"At that time, I was still trying to sort through my anger. The thought of raising my son in an environment where I could possibly blame him was... I just couldn't do it. To have him bear my cross or be reminded that he was a product of rape... I don't know, it just seemed insane to me, you know. I loved him so much, too much to do that."

Tearing his gaze from the fire, Carvin's eyes met mine, "If you could do it all over again, would you have given him up for adoption?"

Staring down at my bare toes, I allowed my right foot to caress my left as I replayed visions of 'what if'. "You know, I've pondered that same question a million times. And, honestly, no. I would have allowed my parents to raise him. They offered numerous times, but I was so afraid. Afraid that I would sabotage his life with my issues. Just young and confused I guess. And, I hate myself for that." As the sheet of Guilt slowly started to shroud me, I found myself descending further under it for refuge. Guilt had become my comfortable place. For years, it accompanied me down memory lane, sharing vivid memories of my first love, never allowing me to forget him. Guilt was both generous with itself and always reliable. Whenever I called, it unselfishly made itself available. Strangely enough, I felt indebted to Guilt for its dedication to keeping the memories alive. Without Guilt, I was afraid I would forget him, so I held on to it even tighter.

As I unknowingly began to pace in front of the fireplace, Carvin proceeded to interrupt my growing anxiety.

"Kendall."

Reaching for my hand, Carvin smiled gently as his stare consoled me. I took another sip of wine and knelt down between his legs, resting my head on his shoulder. "But one thing I was certain of," I continued, "was that he deserved a chance at life and I was determined to give it to him."

"You are a beautiful woman, inside and out. Baby, you must let the guilt go. You need to let it go. Do you recognize your strength and testimony? There are young girls right now who are in a dark place and need to hear your story."

Surrounded by silence, we allowed the fire to serenade and comfort our thoughts. Guilt, offended by his dismissive comment, decided to loosen its grip, allowing Carvin to pull me into a deeper embrace.

Carvin caressed my hands, massaging each finger with a single kiss. After each finger had its share of affection, he circled back to my ring finger. He looked me in the eyes as he gently lured it into his mouth and teased it between his tongue and soft lips. At that moment, my yearning to make love to him pulsated between my thighs. When he released my finger, my desire to love him forever swelled in my heart. Speechless, I stared at my finger, magically adorned with the same sparkling jewel from earlier that night.

"Kendall Marie Johnson, will you marry me? We all have problems baby, that's life. Let's sort through ours together. On my way home, I prayed for God to teach me how to love you. For the rest of my life, I pray God will bless me with the honor of learning how to love and protect every facet of you."

Is this really happening?

"Please, don't make me start begging like Keith Sweat because you know I will."

Carvin stood up, grabbed the empty wine glass, and started impersonating Keith Sweat, making sure to exaggerate every syllable. I started laughing and crying all at once. I didn't know what was more pitiful, his singing or him dancing naked in front of me. Regardless, only a fool would not marry this phenomenal man.

"Despite your horrendous vocal skills and lack of rhythm, it would be my greatest joy and honor to spend a lifetime learning how to love you, Carvin Alexander."

Love is patient, Love is kind… it keeps no record of wrongs. 1 Corinthians 13:4-5 (NKJV)

One of the greatest expressions of love is covering someone when they find the courage to be transparent and vulnerable in your presence.

And you shall know the truth and the truth shall make you free. (John 8:32)

Fourteen

I never thought planning a wedding would be so stressful. As much as I wanted to be knee deep in the development process, I was more than happy to take a back seat to Mom's wedding planning hysteria. Initially, Carvin and I had agreed on an intimate beach ceremony, with the moonlight and shoreline as our decorative pieces. We decided we would not exceed one hundred guests. Yet, even with our decision to have a simple wedding, when I thought about all the involved parts, I was overwhelmed. So, of course, when Mom said she would take my dream and make it a reality, I was relieved to let her take the steering wheel.

Unfortunately, the euphoria was short lived. Soon after she got involved, the guest list tripled to three hundred and our organic venue ended up being a ritzy hotel.

On this day, Mom and I were at a bridal boutique trying on dresses. After the tenth gown, my muscles were tense and my head was pounding. Eager to get me in her idea of the perfect dress, Mom stepped away with the Specialist, only to return with four more. As soon as I saw the gowns, I felt my blood pressure surge as the knots in my stomach tightened. All were princess style designs, despite telling Mom countless times I was going for a fitted mermaid cut. I curtly dismissed the Specialist and turned to Mom with agitation burning through my skin.

"Mom, what can I do to make you understand? This wedding is about me and Carvin. I realize you and Dad didn't have a formal ceremony, but now is not the time to try to relive your dream."

"Kendall Marie, first off, I'm offended you would even think your special day would be used to play out my wedding fantasy! And, secondly—"

"Mom, please! How are you offended? Growing up, whenever we went to a wedding you would always, and I mean *always*, compare it to what you would have done on your wedding day."

With both hands on her hips she interrupted, "And, what's your point?"

"My point is you always talked about having a wedding in a five-star hotel surrounded by glitz and glamour. Oh, and let me not forget that you put special emphasis on being adored by a crowd of at least two hundred guests. You wanted to wear a princess style gown with a tiara. Oh, and you even said your colors would be black, white, and red. And—"

"Okay, okay, okay! I still don't get your point, Kendall Marie…"

"Mom, you have voluntarily changed my venue to the Downtown Ritz Carlton, you keep pressuring me to get a big ol' poufy Cinderella dress and tiara, and you have somehow managed to alter my wedding colors from sage, cappuccino, and cantaloupe to black, pearl, and crimson. I don't know what else to say, it's crystal clear."

"Look, honey, you are my princess and I want your day to be magical. You can't hate me for that. Besides, Carvin seems to be fine with my ideas."

"I never said I hate you, Mom. And, at this point, Carvin could care less if we got married next to Wilber in a barn. I, on the other hand, have always dreamed of a tranquil beach ceremony surrounded by those I'm closest to. That does not include the church usher board, your book club girlfriends, and Dad's golfing buddies. If we can't speak to how they have profoundly impacted our lives, we don't want them at our wedding. And for the one-hundredth time, I don't want to be a princess bride!"

I stepped off the platform and wobbled my way back to the dressing room to get out of the itching mountain of tulle. As the specialist was helping me undress, Mom stepped into the dressing room and asked if she and I could have a moment of privacy. The specialist obliged and left us in silence. Not wanting to argue with Mom further, I chose to ignore her and focused on removing the corset.

"You're right."

Oh, really?

"I didn't realize I was crowding out your vision with mine. I can admit when I'm wrong and I'm sorry."

"Ummhmm, sorry enough to abandon your insane idea of having Great Gammy serve as my flower girl? She is ninety years old, blind, and can barely keep her dentures in. I love Gammy, you know I do, but a flower girl? Really?" Tired of fussing with my corset, I collapsed on the satin covered stool and leaned my head against the mirror. As I waited for Mom's retort, I closed my eyes to relieve the tension mounting between them.

"We've discussed this Ken. Gammy's dying wish is to be in your wedding. Your grandmother and I didn't have formal weddings, none of your great aunts got married, so Gammy never got to relish in the euphoria of being in a wedding. When she asked to be the flower girl, I just couldn't say no."

"So how do you expect her to coordinate getting down the aisle and throwing out rose petals? Gammy can't see, walk, or barely stay awake!"

"Okay, okay you're right. I'll figure out some miraculous way to change her mind. This is my baby girl's special day and I want it to be perfect."

Mom stepped closer and assisted me with removing the veil that had somehow gotten snagged in my hair. Once we released, she sat down on the stool next to me.

"It wasn't until a moment ago that I realized how regretful I am about not having wedding. Your dad and I got married at the local courthouse because we didn't have parents who could afford a ceremony. With us being so young, we were too penniless to afford one. Anyway, I'm really sorry, sweetheart."

I turned around and embraced Mom. There was no way I could stay mad at her, especially since I knew all her efforts and motives stemmed from a place of love. Besides, I was most relieved to know she wasn't chewing me out for raising my voice.

"Mom, you don't have to apologize for anything."

"Yes, I do and so do you."

"Huh?" I leaned back with raised brows.

"Don't think I'm going to allow you to raise your voice at me without checking you on it!"

I burst out laughing. "Checking me on it? Mom, you don't even talk like that." Hearing Mrs. Prim and Proper get street on me was the highlight of the day. "But you're right. I was wrong for raising my voice at you and I'm sorry. Please forgive me?" I pinched her cheeks and started tickling her side to lighten the mood.

Mom rolled her eyes and then kissed me on the cheek. "Of course, I forgive my pumpkin! Now let's finish getting you out of this dress so we can go gorge on wedding cake. I made a taste testing appointment for today at three."

"Oh no, I can't today. I need to run into the office to finish up an article and then meet Carvin for dinner. I'm sorry. Dang, I wish you would have told me sooner."

"You're always just pushing your old mom aside. That's okay. Your dad and I can go and pretend like we're getting married. That always seems to get him excited."

"Wait, so when did you and Dad start engaging in illegal activity?"

"Well, the last time you stood me up for the dinner tasting, I called your dad, and he met me at the caterers. We had a blast! We were fat-full by the time we rolled out."

"They didn't charge you or ask for ID?" I asked, still confused.

"No, and if they did, we would have kindly educated them on who's paying for this wedding. I guarantee, once they realize the money is coming from your daddy's wallet, they won't give a dolphin's big toenail about who we are."

"A dolphin's big toenail? Really, Mom? You went from hood to prude in less than five minutes." We both laughed and embraced again.

By this time, the specialist returned and politely inserted herself into our space to continue removing my gown. I could tell by Mom's facial expression that she was perturbed by her abrupt interruption of our intimate moment. Before Mom could say anything further, I shooed her out of the dressing room. The last thing I needed was for her to try and 'check' the woman.

Before you ridicule someone for their actions, take a moment and try to identify the motive and/or intention behind their efforts. Someone's love for you may not always manifest the way you expect. If you recognize it's from a sincere place, find the strength to extend grace and patience.

Fifteen

With the dresses off, and my signature black leggings and tank top on, I tucked my shoulder length tresses under my favorite Kango hat and headed to meet my mom outside the boutique entrance. After enduring a morning of dress shopping, I popped Tylenols like skittles to help suppress my inner Bridezilla. To avoid another confrontation with my mom, I hugged her farewell and limped my tired feet to the car.

Carvin had planned a nice dinner date for that evening, but with it being after one o'clock, I was afraid if I didn't get started on my article, I would be late. Fortunately, I worked in Midtown, which was not far from the bridal boutique. That ten-minute ride would give me enough time to call Carrie to find out about her first month as a mommy.

"Hey, Carrie! I miss you, mamacita. How are you and baby Jackson doing?"

"Aww, Ken! I miss ya more. Baby Jackson is doing wonderful. Girl, I'm so in love with him. It's kinda bad, but I keep forgetting I have a husband. Jacky pooh is all I think about." Carrie cooed into the phone, as she proceeded to whisper baby talk to Jackson.

"How precious. I need to see him and get some of his sweet kisses. But, poor Miles! Where is he now?"

"He's lying on my chest, staring up at me. He probably wants some of this liquid gold. He's so beautiful, Ken. He's my little Pookie pie."

"Wait, what? Oh lawd! Girl, not Jackson, your husband! Where is Miles?"

"Oh! Oops. Miles is in his man cave laughing at crazy Dave Chappelle."

"That's a shame Carrie." I shook my head in disbelief as I tried to merge onto 59N toward Downtown. Although Houston sunshine was like no other, the rainstorm of traffic always had a way of disturbing a perfectly good day.

"What did you say?" Carrie softly asked, clearly still entertaining baby Jack.

"I said that's a shame that you do your husband like that!"

"Oh yeah. I know. I really need to do better. What is all that noise in the background, I can barely hear ya?"

"Oh, my air conditioner went out last week, so I have to drive with my windows down. I made an appointment with my mechanic to—"

"Please, don't say anotha word. I can't take it anymore, Ken! Can ya please get a new car! We have an extra car ya can use. I can't have my diva driving around in that piece of junk. That ain't kosha!"

My family and friends always joked about my old and tired Cherry Pie. My 1995 red Toyota Camry was begging to be delivered from her misery and released to car heaven. Whenever my radio decided to work, it competed with the moans and groans of the engine. Even worse, my driver side door didn't open from the outside and the trunk wouldn't always lock properly. Plenty of times, I came to an abrupt stop and my trunk flew open. The worst times were when it happened at a busy intersection. It never failed; I would get out of my car and close the driver side door, forgetting it was broken. After I closed the trunk, I'd have to climb into the car from the passenger side, subjecting myself to glares from impatient drivers as they honked or drove around me. Carvin, utterly disgusted by my car, threatened to sell her every time he rode with me, which was rare. Despite its idiosyncrasies, I loved Cherry Pie and refused to let her go until after the wedding.

"Like I've said in the past, I'm going to ride my Cherry until she pops. With the wedding coming up and school loans kicking my butt, the last thing I'm concerned about is a new car and new car payments. I'm not trying to be rude, but shouldn't you be worried about your man and not my car?"

"Oh, I see ya checked me real quick! But ya right. Before ya called, Miles was lying next to me, complaining that I hadn't said anything kinky or affectionate to him in the last month. I feel horrible, girl. I mean, I've been so caught up with baby Jack, I guess I lost my mojo."

"I assume that's expected, right? I can see how that might be a bit normal after the baby is born."

"Sure, but when we said our vows, we promised we wouldn't have an average marriage. Now, Miles has kept his word. He still compliments me when I know I look like a hippopotamus. He massages my feet and brings me breakfast in the morning. Girl, he even washes my vagina every night."

"Carrie, seriously! You can't wash your own kitty kat?"

"Did ya forget I suffered twenty-seven hours of labor and gave birth to a nine-pound six-ounce baby boy? My poor va-jay-jay was traumatized. Now, let's not get it twisted, my honey is well endowed, but he's no competition for nine pounds of baby fat!"

Slowly, I exhaled, shaking my head in embarrassment as if the drivers next to me could hear the details of Carrie's confessions. "Ummm, wow. Okay. Too much information, way too much…"

"Oh, whateva, girl. Ya grown. And, besides, with baby Jack on my breasts all day and all this extra weight, I can't even find my vagina half the time. But, I wouldn't expect y'all ladies without children to understand the plight of motherhood..." Carrie's voice trailed off.

Without saying a word, I already knew what she was thinking. After the fiasco at my surprise birthday party, both Jasmine and Carrie had been extremely cautious when talking about babies or motherhood around me.

"I'm so sorry, Ken. I hope I didn't offend ya or, um, I uh..."

Luckily, I had just pulled into the parking garage, the perfect excuse to halt any further discussion. "Carrie, it's okay. Believe me, I'm fine. I don't want you feeling like I'm some emotionally fragile nutcase. I'm fine."

"Okay, it's just... Are ya sure?"

"Yes, I'm positive. Look, I'm at the office and really need to finish this article before date night with Carvin. I'm glad to hear you and baby Jack are doing good. I'll try to make it by this weekend to see you all. Promise me when we hang up you'll go talk nasty to your man!"

"Okay, now ya starting to sound like Jasmine! But, sure, I can do that. Love ya, Ken."

"Love you, too, Carrie. I'll try to call you tomorrow."

"Okay, baby, Jack and I would like that. Bye."

"Bye."

As I hung up the phone, my heart was quickly flooded with the beats of grief. Hearing Carrie talk about her adoration for baby Jack made me recall the night I met my first love. Not wanting to lose time reminiscing, I inhaled deeply and exhaled as I grabbed my purse, got out of the car, and headed toward the office.

At my desk, I kicked off my heels, took off my hat, and put on my favorite jazz artist, R. Nelson. Before turning on my laptop, I leaned back in my chair and whispered a quick prayer for focus and productivity.

"Dear God, thank you so much for Your love and faithfulness. As I prepare to complete my latest article, I ask that Your favor goes before me and creates a path of success. I pray over my ability to focus and be productive during the next several hours. I dedicate my work and my efforts to You. Please allow Your strength, wisdom, knowledge, and understanding to lead and guide my every step. Amen. Oh, wait, and one more thing, God. I pray over my son. Wherever he is, I pray that he is happy, safe, healthy, and loved. Kiss him for me. Amen."

With my laptop booted up and R. Nelson serenading me, I allowed myself to get lost in my work. As expected, whenever I prayed and surrendered a project, situation, or issue to God, He would show up and show out.

As I completed the final edits, I beamed with pride at my finished product. I forwarded my article to Andy Williams, turned off my laptop, and gathered my purse, ready to get sexy for date night. As I reached for my phone, I was alarmed to see that I had ten missed calls and several text messages from Carvin. It wasn't until I looked at my watch that I realized the reason for the calls. It was seven forty-five and I was supposed to meet Carvin for dinner at six… Shoot!

As I sprinted to the car, I mustered up the courage to call Carvin back and plead for his forgiveness. With each ring, my courage dissipated and by the time he finally answered, I had lost all valor to speak.

"Kendall, where are you?" he barked.

Startled, I jolted, dropping my phone between the driver seat and driver side door. "Huh…?"

As I reached for the phone, I heard Carvin blowing out a loud breath of frustration. "What do you mean 'huh'? I have been trying to reach you for over two hours and that's all you have to say?"

"I know, I'm sorry. I've been in the office this whole time completing my article and the time escaped me. I forgot I turned off the volume on my phone, which explains the missed calls. I'm so sorry, babe! We can still do dinner and catch a late movie."

"That's not the point, Kendall!" Carvin released another exasperated sigh. "The dinner was just a disguise to get you to meet me at the Justice of the Peace. I know I was initially against us eloping and all, but I've seen the stress this wedding has been causing you. I made an appointment for us to have an intimate ceremony at the courthouse, just you and me. My Uncle David, the presiding judge, was going to marry us."

"Oh, babe, are you serious? Wow, I'm so, so, so sorry! Do you think he can do it tomorrow?"

"I already inquired, and he can't do it this week. I'll ask him about sometime later this month. Man, you know how to mess up plans."

"I know, I suck. Can I make it up to you?"

After what seemed like a nine-month pregnant pause, Carvin cleared his throat, "Hmmm, let me think. Keep talking…"

"Meet me at the Marriott off Westheimer. I will have on a black lace dress with red pumps. My hair will be pinned back. When you approach me, be sure to address me as Lolita." I could sense Carvin smiling on the other end as he contemplated my proposal. Although stubborn, one thing he loved was role-playing, so I was confident this would soften him up.

"Ken, you really know how to keep a brotha! I thought you wanted to keep your purse closed until the wedding night. Opening it up just might cost you some serious change."

He was right, but I was feeling frisky and naughty.

"Exactly! My purse is closed, but I have a few other pockets you might be able to pull a few coins out of…"

"Aaaahhhh…" It sounded like Carvin was licking his lips. "I see. Well, tell Lolita Mr. Armstrong will meet her at the bar in an hour. Don't be late."

With that, he hung up. Thank God I packed my clothes for this evening, so that would save some time. I grabbed my overnight bag, dashed out of my car and back into the office to change.

As luck would have it, I lost all my change and it was worth every penny. In the hotel elevator, I'm sure we gave the eyes behind the security camera a visual treat as I invited his hands to massage between my thighs and his tongue between my lips. Once in the room, we slid to the floor and made love up against the door. We eventually crawled to the bed and continued tasting, eating, and absorbing our love for the rest of the evening.

After six months of no sex, I felt like a virgin again. Although remorseful the next morning, I couldn't blame Carvin. He tried to refrain, but Lolita was on fire and he had easily fallen prey to her heat. We decided, yet again, that we would hold off until our actual wedding night. Until then, I knew I needed serious prayer!

Allowing others to dictate your life can be burdensome. Have the courage to follow your own vision, even when others can't see it.

Prayer is an intimate invitation for God's presence to be present in your life. Pray without ceasing, and expect to see Him Show Up and Show Out!

Life Lesson

Sixteen

It had been over three months since Carvin and I had our sexual escapade and, to my surprise, we had found the strength to remain abstinent. The only issue we were having these days was Mom.

The wedding was approximately three months away and Mom had completely disregarded the heart-to-heart we had months ago. Although she tolerated my desired colors, she neglected to cancel the reservation at the Ritz Carlton. Despite promising it was an oversight on her behalf, I found that difficult to believe. Priding herself on being organized and focused, there was no way she accidentally forgot; that was an anomaly in her world. In addition, the guest list somehow increased to three hundred and Gammy was still in the bridal party. I had come to terms that my flower girl may not make it down the aisle before I do.

Despite how disturbing that may be, the most horrific truth had nothing to do with Mom and her mania, but all to do with me. During my final dress fitting, I was flabbergasted to find out my dress had shrunk one size. With weekly, hot yoga and cycling classes, my seamstress' announcement of my invisible weight gain left me hysterical. If anything, I was expecting to hear her say my gown would need to be taken in. Even more disappointing was the necessary alterations would cost almost as much as the dress.

"This is ridiculous! I've been denying myself food and working out like the Incredible Hulk and you have the nerve to tell me my dress is too small!"

"Ms. Johnson, I can certainly understand your frustration—"

"Please don't patronize me. You have *no* idea how I feel right now. No idea!" I brushed past the seamstress and grabbed a Kleenex from her antique wooden desk. Between perspiration soaking my body and the tears violating my face, I was ready to scream.

"I apologize, you're right. Have you had any recent changes to your diet or been harboring any stress? I've found in the past that our brides will retain water due to stress or high salt diet weeks prior to the wedding. If you want—"

"Ma'am, I don't intend to be disrespectful, but *clearly* you're not listening to me. I just told you I've been a self-inflicted anorexic these past few months. I just… Ugh!"

In an attempt to arrest my flailing arms, Mom grabbed my hands and sat me down on the red stiletto-shaped sofa. "Kendall, calm down. You can have the dress altered and it will be ready before your special day. Your dramatic chants are unnecessary. You're acting like a heathen in here and that is *not* ladylike."

"Mom, I love you, but this is not the time or place." As I massaged my temples, I turned back to the seamstress, inhaling deeply. "I'm sorry, but Ms.—. Please remind me of your name."

"Ms. Clarke."

"Ms. Clarke, I appreciate your patience and assistance, I really do. Is it possible this is not my dress? Did you mistakenly sell my dress to someone else? I really, really find it hard to believe my dress doesn't fit."

Choosing not to mirror my frustration, Ms. Clarke kindly responded, "No, Ms. Johnson. This is your dress."

"Are you sure?" I stood up and faced the mirrors, desperately searching the dress for evidence that it belonged to another bride. The vintage lace sweetheart neckline struggled to keep my breast tamed, while my hips and butt tried to bully their way out. As much as the dress and I tried to control my assets, their stubbornness won.

"Yes ma'am. I'm confident this is your dress."

"Ummmhmmm.... Well, I'm not. Can I please speak to the boutique owner or the CEO?"

Ms. Clarke cleared her throat and smiled. "That would be me."

Drained by my tantrum, Mom quickly interjected. "Kendall Marie, that is enough! This is your dress! Now I am tired of this tirade. What has gotten into you? Are you going to purchase a new dress or have this one altered? I'm sure there is another bride who would love this dress if you don't want it."

"Why would I give *my* dress away? This is *my* dress and to give it away to another bride is not an option. I've been preparing for months for this dress... *my* dress," I cried out.

"Well then keep your dress and toss the attitude. Your indignant behavior is uncouth and downright embarrassing." Rolling her eyes, Mom turned to the seamstress. "Ms. Clarke, please accept my apologies."

Mom was right. Scanning the small boutique, the brides and their guests resembled mannequins staring in my direction. *What was wrong with me?* I knew the dress was mine, but I was embarrassed to know I had allowed myself to eat my way out of it. When I contemplated my eating habits over the past several months, the invisible weight gain made no sense. I took a moment to exhale and observe my frame in the array of mirrors. As of recent, I felt like my five-foot-eight-inch frame carried less weight. My thighs and stomach appeared to have gone down. Yes, my breast and booty were suppler, but without Carvin gawking over them I would have never noticed. As for the territorial outbursts, I already knew the culprit. I felt a cool draft as the smooth sheet of Guilt started its ascent up my back legs. Before I could slide it up further, a river of tears trickled down my cheeks, softening my pride. I apologized to Ms. Clarke for my abnormal behavior, pleading for her forgiveness. I assured her the extra money for the alterations would somehow be provided.

Fortunately, Ms. Clark forgave me for my childish rant and blessed me with a twenty-five percent discount on the alteration fee. Amazed at her reaction, I inquired why and her response left me speechless.

"Sweetie, displacing your anger and frustration on me comes with the job. After twenty-five years of serving in this industry, I've learned to tolerate the Bridezillas that grace my boutique. But, what I don't often see is a bride gather herself and ask for my forgiveness. It's hard to admit fault and apologize, especially when strangers are watching. If you bring that attitude into marriage, I know you'll be happily married for your lifetime."

"Wow, if anything, I expected you to ban me, my attitude, and these extra pounds from your boutique. Thank you, Ms. Clarke, for excusing my ways. I will certainly try to live by your wise words. Lord knows my Carvin would be grateful."

"And that he will. Now, let's make this dress perfect."

With church service and the dress fitting behind us, we decided to spend the rest of our Sunday afternoon preparing an old-fashioned Southern feast. Since cooking was not a skill of mine, I cherished these intimate learning moments. Mom floating around the kitchen like a chef goddess, turning simple ingredients into grandiose cuisines, reminded me of my beautiful childhood. Although both worked outside the home, my parents prided themselves on creating a rich lifestyle for me and Kenton. While pursuing a successful career as a college professor, Mom always found the time to cook a delicious meal, help us with our homework, and support our extracurricular activities. As a high-ranking Captain in the Navy, Dad was a genius at balancing a militant work life and a loving, orderly household.

The menu for tonight included bacon wrapped hen, squash dressing, mustard greens, caramel glazed yams, macaroni and cheese, potato salad, and her homemade honey raisin rolls. I was in Heaven.

"Tell me about work, honey. Last we talked you were stressed out about your latest project. I can't remember all of the details, but I thought you said it had something to do with traveling overseas to document poverty?"

Mom stepped inside the walk-in pantry to gather all her spices, while I updated her on the woes of my job.

"I wish I was going overseas. I've been working at this agency for close to three years and every single time an international project comes up I'm overlooked. I'm the best photographer at our firm. After traveling all around the United States, documenting the homeless and training several of our interns only to see them get promoted, I can't help but feel unappreciated. I'm ready for more now."

"More importantly, you deserve more, sweetheart." Mom returned from the pantry and started reaching for her pots hanging above the island. "If you're ready for more, and it's evident you are, the resounding question is what's holding you back?"

"The leadership, or lack thereof! How many more stories can I follow about homelessness in the states? I need to grow beyond

Brooklyn, Chicago, San Francisco, and Houston. For instance, just last month we had an opportunity open for a photojournalist to chronicle the plaguing poverty in Haiti. Would you believe Andy had the audacity to give it to our newest intern? The intern that I spent all summer training!"

"Okay," Mom responded while meticulously lining her spices in order on the island.

"Okay... Am I the only one that see's the injustices being rendered here?" With my arms up in disbelief, I looked around the kitchen, further emphasizing my point.

"Kendall Marie, we have had this discussion several times and you always shy away from answering the same question I always present, 'What is holding you back and what are you going to do about it?' It's obvious Andy is not going to change."

Mom handed me the dough, motioned for me to start kneading it, and started washing the greens in the sink. "One thing I did *not* do was raise you or your brother to live a victimized life. Situations are not always going to be ideal or favorable, honey. Sometimes, you must create the perfect opportunity. I realize you are unhappy right now, so find creative ways to make your current job your dream job, until that dream job presents itself."

Insulted by Mom's accusations, I pushed the half-kneaded dough aside and sulked over to the glass-topped breakfast table. It was a beautiful day outside and the sun shining through the wall length window provided comfort for the cold shade I felt her shooting my way. I curled up in the wooden seat like a wounded kitten. "I like how you've made it my fault. I've tried. Whenever these international opportunities are presented, I always apply and voice my interest to Andy. I'm vocal about what I want. I can't help it if my words fall on deaf ears."

"Victim," Mom stated matter-of-factly.

"What?"

"Victim. There you go resigning yourself to be the victim. Have you ever thought about researching opportunities before they are presented? Identify a poverty-stricken country that has not been showcased by the firm and write up a brief article, illustrating your findings. Create a proposal, highlighting how your involvement would be beneficial to the firm and what will be necessary to make it a reality. Hand over the article and proposal to your boss and see what happens. Ken, I need you to be several steps ahead and create the opportunity for yourself. The whining has to stop."

"It's not that easy—"

Mom slammed her empty pot down on the granite countertop, as she exhaled, staring out the window above the sink. "It is that easy! How do you think I became a tenured professor?"

Before I could think of an answer, Mom turned away from the window and started cutting the yams. She stopped for a moment and looked at me, shaking her head. "When I realized all the appointments were going to my less than qualified colleagues, I was livid. There were many nights I burned your dad's ears with my fiery tirades and blazing expletives about how I was being mistreated. Finally, he asked me the same questions I'm asking you. At that moment, I chose to focus on my drive for success. I became intentional about my grants, identifying research protocols that had not been exhausted or attempted by my colleagues. I allowed my hunger for justice to fuel my creativity and actions. At times, did I still want to sulk and whine about it? Of course! But, with prayer and the support of your dad, I found the courage to act. You see, Kendall, life gifts you 86,400 seconds every day to either complain and remain or take second steps toward the life you were created to live."

Eager to prove my point, I retorted, "Exactly, and I've been taking second step after second step, without any results."

"But you've also been complaining at the same time. The two can't coexist without canceling each other out, darling."

I turned from staring out the window to Dad entering the kitchen with a bouquet of gladiolas for Mom. "Your mom knows what she's talking about. You've been complaining for the past year about feeling overlooked and underappreciated. What's holding you back and what are you going to do about it?"

Peering over her favorite apple red, cat-eyed glasses, like only an educator would do, Mom gave me a wink that screamed, *I told you so.*

"Let's see, stop complaining? I don't know. You all make it seem so easy. I don't know what else to do."

"That's just it. You just cited the answer." Dad stood in the middle of the kitchen, darting his eyes at me and then at Mom, and back at me as if to say, *So, why are we having this discussion again?*

"Huh? I did... What? Okay, enough with the da Vinci code antics, just tell me what to do. I'm exhausted with trying to figure out the riddle."

Mom shook her head as she grabbed the flowers from Dad and started to arrange them in the crystal centerpiece adorning the island. "I swear I didn't raise no fools, but sometimes I find myself wondering. Girl, stop complaining! That's the answer. Challenge yourself to act without complaining."

"Oh. Has it really gotten that bad?" I said with a slight grin.

"Yes!" Mom and Dad chimed in unison.

"Well, don't be so enthusiastic about it. But, I suppose you might be a little bit right. Especially about creating my own opportunities."

Dad smiled at Mom and nodded to me in agreement. He walked over and kissed me on the forehead. "Well, I guess we didn't raise a fool after all. I knew my baby girl had some common sense. Now, your brother...the jury is still out on that nutcase." Dad laughed to himself as he headed to the theatre room to indulge in Sunday Night Football.

"All right, Garfield and friends, enough sunbathing in the window. Come help your mom over here in the kitchen. You and your brother better take advantage of my cooking skills while you have me on this earth."

I peeled myself away from the window, playfully tickling her as I walked past her to the island.

"Thanks, Mom."

"Of course, honey. Don't thank me with words. Thank me through your actions."

"I think I can do that. I'll start by not complaining about the fact that Gammy is still my flower girl. Yep, I won't complain." I looked away, trying to hide my smile as she threw the dish towel in my direction.

"You keep talking smart and I just might ask Uncle Bart to be the ring bearer. Since getting out of jail, you know he loves to stash away shiny things."

We both busted out laughing as I attempted to knead the dough. "Okay, you win. Last time I saw him he tried to steal the silver door handles off my car. That's when I knew at least one other person saw the value in my hoopty."

One of the hardest things to do is admit when you are wrong and apologize, especially in the company of others. That's a mutually beneficial expression of humility.

Life gifts you 86,400 seconds every day to either complain or take second steps toward change. The two can't coexist without canceling each other out. Which will you choose?

Until you decide to hold yourself accountable for your current situation and empower yourself toward change, you will always remain a victim.

Seventeen

The first few times Carrie called me crying about feeling fat and depressed, I dismissed it as overreacting and seeking attention. Heralded for her striking beauty and slender build, after Carrie had the baby, I expected her to encounter a few bumps trying to reconnect with her additional thirty pounds.

It wasn't until she started stalking my phone that I recognized there was a true problem. Twenty times within a twenty-four-hour period was a record. Each time I reluctantly answered, Carrie greeted me with wails about her broken marriage and excessive weight gain.

On one particular day, by the twentieth phone call, I decided to call Miles to get to the bottom of her manic behavior. Gym bag in hand, I bid farewell to my hot yoga buddies and headed toward my car. With my mind, body, and spirit clear, there was no better time than the present to call Miles up to discuss an intervention.

"For real Kendall, I don't know what's up with your girl these days. She's trippin'. Despite all my efforts, I can't do anything right!" Miles shouted.

"Well, she has called me close to twenty times, crying about you looking at 'skinny ho's' behind her back and refusing to make love to her. She even left me a message stating she was jealous about the relationship you have with the baby. I mean, what in the world is going on?"

"Personally, I think she is experiencing late onset postpartum depression. I do all I can to make sure Carrie knows my heart belongs to her—"

"And you always have," I reassured Miles.

"Uh, well yeah, at least you can see that. Lately, with her my actions go unnoticed. I'm serious; your boy needs some guidance. I don't know what else to do. When I ask her about going to see a therapist, she gets pissed. I try to make love to her and she obsesses about her vagina lips being too black and her butt too fat. Hell, I love anything black and PHAT, that's the perfect combo!"

Immediately, I pull the phone away as my shoulders and mouth cringe, "Wait, what? Even in a crazed state, she's hilarious. And please, way too much info bro!"

"Sorry. I'm just saying Kendall. I think you and Jasmine need to get together and do a serious intervention. Baby Jack and I can go spend Saturday with my parents. Feel free to come over and do what you do.... I miss my wife, Ken, and I will do anything to make it right again. I need your help."

"Of course, Jas and I got you. Not sure there's much we can do, but with prayer and several glasses of Merlot, I'm sure we can bring our girl back to life. You provide the wine and food, and we'll bring the prayer and therapy."

"Deal! I might need to add a few bottles of Hennessey and Tequila up in the mix too... Man, my baby needs something strong."

"Well, all right now! I just arrived at the salon. I'll follow up with you later this week to confirm the details. Call me if you need anything."

"Will do. Thanks, Ken."

"Anytime, Miles."

That following Friday I met up with Jas to discuss our game plan for the weekend rescue mission. I hadn't seen my best friend in a couple of weeks, so I was excited to get a dose of her over some smooth grooves and cocktails.

As always, I was the first to arrive. I scouted out a nice, intimate booth right next to the stage and summoned the fine waiter to get the first round of drinks flowing. As he flirtatiously finalized my order, I looked toward the entrance to see my beautiful friend strutting my way, adorned in her infamous black pencil skirt and yellow chiffon button down blouse.

"Hey Jasmine! Oh, how I've missed you. Thanks for suggesting Styles tonight; you know I love the live music here. With work kicking my butt, I've been looking forward to this sexy saxophone serenading my stress away."

We embrace as I kiss her on the cheek and motion for the waiter to return.

"You already know girl! *Oh*, I'm loving your red halter dress. Very classy, with just enough sass." Jasmine winked at me as she scooted into the booth.

"Thanks, love. I may stick to leggings and tanks when I'm chilling, but when it's time to step out, I know how to bring it!" We gave each other a high five as the waiter returned with our drinks and fried calamari.

"So, work is still stressing my girl, huh? Maybe it's time to throw them the deuces. You're too talented, Ken. I hate seeing you sell yourself for scraps. You already know I'll leave a job in a second honey. As a matter of fact, I'm no longer slaving at Trust Bank."

"Wait! What? I thought you were lining yourself up for Vice President of Marketing. You invested so much over the past three years in preparation for this opportunity."

"Exactly! But, we know the politics of our male dominated corporate America. Can you believe they had the nerve to give the position to Ditzy Debbie?"

I leaned in closer to Jas to be certain I heard her correctly, "Excuse me? The same Ditzy Debbie, who thought sea horses were actual horses with gills?"

"Yes girl, that's the one!" Jas hissed, rolling her eyes to the ceiling to emphasize her disdain.

With widened eyes, I continued. "Do you remember when you last invited her to your place for ladies night and I offered her one of my Nestlé's chocolate turtles?"

"Oh snap! Girl yes, I almost forgot. When she responded, 'No thanks, I'm a vegetarian', I had to run and get a mirror so you could fix your face. That was a crazy evening." We stared at each other with silly grins plastered across our face as we silently recalled the epic night.

"But, wait! I thought she was sleeping with the CEO?" I took another sip of Merlot as I tried to rinse away the shock.

"Yeah, well she sucked all of the brain out of his damn head, no pun intended, and he couldn't think straight. Girl, I wish you were at the meeting when he made the announcement. I almost took off this stiletto and beat his ass with it. My gosh, I was so pissed!" Jas took off one of her cheetah print stilettos and imitated beating him with it.

"Understandably so. I'm so sorry, Jas."

"Sorry, for what? Girl, please. No need to apologize. Unlike you, I refuse to give away my time and talents to a company who doesn't appreciate me."

Immediately, I cupped my right cheek to mimic the pain of a slap. "Well slap the truth across my face!"

"Am I lying?" Jas asked as she tilted her head to one side and slanted her lips to the other, waiting for my answer.

"Well, for your information I'm working on a proposal to document the poverty ailing Eritrea. I'm hoping to link up with this startup non-profit and illustrate their efforts. I have one in mind; I just need to make my proposal so convincing that Andy has no choice, but to say yes."

"And if she says no?"

"My resignation will follow shortly after. I've already discussed it with Carvin and he supports me taking a few months off to seek out another position."

Jasmine lifted her glass of Cabernet in the air and beckoned for me to do the same, "Well, let's toast to that. It's about damn time, Ken. They truly underestimate you. And, that Andy, she is deranged. Cruella Devil needs a man, a girl, a she-man, something. I swear that chick is a lipstick lesbian in the closet."

"Yes, cheers to me creating the life I desire and getting the recognition I deserve. As for your other statement, no comment." Reaching for a mouth full of calamari, I continue, "So, let's talk about our sista girl Carrie."

"Oh wow." Jasmine leaned back, crossed her arms, and stared at me as her mahogany stained lips formed into a smile.

"What?" I respond sincerely confused.

"No complaining on and on about work." She took another sip of wine and continued to smile, "I'm proud of you. I see progress." We lifted our wine glasses again and chimed them in honor of my growth.

"Thanks girl. I'm really trying to change my attitude and approach with work. I've been doing the same thing for too long and expecting different results. The only variable I can control is me. This may sound crazy, but I am *finally* starting to get it. Anyhow, let's talk about what truly matters. What are we going to do about Carrie? I'm really worried."

"It's simple. We're going to overwhelm her with love and support, while filling her up with drinks, girl. I think she just needs a night of liquor and laughter with her girls. I would go crazy in a house with my husband and newborn too. Hence, why I'm single and barren." Jasmine sashayed her arms in the air to emphasize her point.

"You're crazy! And, you're right, she needs some laughter. We just have to be prepared if our intervention doesn't work. If she is truly suffering from postpartum depression, she will need immediate medical attention. Prayerfully that won't be the case."

"Love conquers all, Kendall. No need to stress, we will get her through this. Don't be mad, but I have a date meeting me here, and I believe he just showed up." Jas looked past me and licked her lips at the tall, well-dressed Asian guy at the entrance. He walked toward us, never taking his penetrating gaze off her.

I looked back at Jas to find her gazing at him and biting her bottom lip as she whispers, "Ooowee, I think I know what I want to eat. Or, who I want to eat me."

As the handsome gentleman approached our booth, she introduced him without breaking her stare, "Ken meet Bolton, Bolton meet Ken."

"Hi, nice to meet you, Bolton." I kindly responded, as my outstretched hand was left unacknowledged. "So, I guess I'll leave you two to screw while I head home and make love to my fiancé." I was hoping my bold statement would snap them out of their trance.

Jasmine winked at me as she sensually scooted out of the booth into her suitor's embrace. "Sure, okay, Ken. You get home safely and I'll see you tomorrow."

Without another word, I swallowed the rest of my drink, grabbed my clutch, and headed to valet, leaving Jas and her date to their sexual tango. Since she chose to cut our date short, I intentionally left my bill for her play toy to pay.

The next afternoon, I showed up to Carrie's house surprised to find Jas already there. One thing Jas was committed to was being late. I was even more amazed when a vibrant and glamorous Carrie greeted me. I had already prepared myself to find her balled up on the floor wearing a moo-moo, with sunken eyes, and a nappy nest on her head.

"Hey, divas! Oh, my gosh, Carrie, you look beautiful!"

"What did ya expect? I might be an emotional mess, but I always make sure I stay fly. Besides, Jasmine came over early to do my hair and makeup." Carrie twirled around to show a three-sixty-degree view of her transformation.

Now her house was the complete contrast. Dirty dishes and old food adorned her contemporary style kitchen. The mahogany wood floors had turned into a garden of dirty clothes and crumbs.

Disgusted by the disarray, I spoke before I could police my words. "You look gorgeous, but your house looks like it's going through postpartum depression! Carrie, this is a mess!" As we followed Carrie to her master bedroom, I continued to take inventory of the disorder, crying out for relief, secretly praying Jasmine and I hadn't bitten off more than we could chew.

"I know, I know. Jas has already teased me about it. I'm so overwhelmed with the baby and trying to be the perfect wife. I don't know…I just lost myself ya know. And I've found that the easiest thing for me to do is nothing at all." Carrie immediately retreated into a crying frenzy and the emotional drama queen Miles had warned me of started to emerge.

"I'm just tired, ya know. I am so, so tired. I can't do this. Sometimes I just want to… I just want to let it all go and do nothing at all. I feel fat and ugly. I'm too embarrassed to have sex with Miles. Does that make me a terrible wife and mother?" As we sat on Carrie's California king bed, she stared at Jas and me, desperately looking for reassurance.

"Well, guess what? Tonight is your night. Kendall and I are here to give you a break girl. We will clean up while you just sit back and get drunk. Girl, you're a phenomenal mother and wife, so this is our gift to you for all that you do." Jasmine glanced over at me for validation, but the idea of trying to clean up her kitchen, let alone the whole house, was distracting me, "Kendall…"

"Huh? Oh, I'm sorry. Yeah, Jasmine is right, Carrie. You need to be more forgiving and gentle with yourself honey. Let's start with some shots while Jas tells us why she left me hanging last night for this fine dude. Yeah, you thought I forgot!" Reaching over to hug Carrie, I rolled my eyes at Jasmine.

Carrie collapsed into my hug, never taking her swollen eyes off Jasmine. "Yes, just what the doctor ordered, drinks and drama. Thanks, ladies. Y'all two are truly God-sent tonight. So, spill it, Jas, tell me about ya raunchy date."

Five hours, four rounds of shots, three bottles of wine, and eleven slices of pizza later, we had managed not to clean up the master bedroom, only moving our laughter session to the master bathroom. To label us drunk would have been an understatement. We were plastered. Fortunately, Jasmine and I had managed to succeed at one thing, making Carrie laugh.

"So, you mean to tell me you and Carvin have not had sex the entire engagement? *Shit!*" Jas slurred.

"Uh, yeah," I snapped back, as I leaned against the marble Jacuzzi tub, picking at the crust on my last slice of pizza.

"Ya lying, Ken. Ya so lying! Ya nose is only gonna get bigger before the wedding, so ya might want to tell the truth now. I'd hate for ya to mess up y'all wedding photos." Carrie grabbed several tampons from the cabinet underneath the sink and held them up to her nose to emphasize her point.

"Whatever, Carrie," I retorted.

"Carrie is right. I know you've been riding that stallion. His fine ass, girl, please. I wish I would deny my future husband some punani."

I threw the pizza crust at Jasmine, hoping to distract her from the brewing interrogation. "Whatever, Jasmine."

"Prove it!" Carrie shouted, pointing a tampon in my face while holding another to her nose.

"Huh? With a tampon? Girl, stop putting that thing in my face." I swatted Carries arm, which didn't take much effort.

"When I first suspected I was pregnant, I purchased like twenty pregnancy tests. I swear; I was so freakin paranoid. I still have several unda the sink. We triple, double, quadruple dare ya to take a test."

"First off, I don't need to take a test to prove *anything*. Secondly... Secondly... Dang, what was I going to say? Oh, secondly, I'm clearly too drunk to pee straight on that thingy." I huffed.

By this time, we were laid out on the hardwood floor in her restroom, barely able to keep our eyes open. There was no way I could take a pregnancy test. Besides, I knew pregnancy was not a concern of mine. We had a minor slip up, but not extravagant enough to tell my girls about it.

"If you squat, Carrie will hold you up and I will put that stick between your legs. What do you have to hide, boo? Those thick thighs and swollen breast of yours making me think you might have a special delivery real soon!" Jasmine teased.

"Ya are a lil thick Ken."

"Ugh! Rude! Okay, okay. Jeeze, you two are so worrisome."

After an hour of trying to get me on the toilet and coordinated enough to pee on the stick, we halfway succeeded. Exhausted by our efforts, Carrie and Jasmine crashed on the floor, while I remained bent over on the toilet.

The next morning, we found the strength to get Carrie nestled in bed and proceeded to finish the cleaning we failed to complete the night before. By mid-afternoon, we had managed to clean away most of the mess tormenting her home and fragrance her kitchen with baked chicken, mashed potatoes, greens, and corn bread.

Carrie slowly shuffled into the kitchen, wrapped in her robe and a towel draped over her forehead. Moaning with each step, she gasped at the transformation in her house. "Thank ya so much, Jas and Ken. Y'all have no idea how much this means to me. As for last night, I have no idea what we did, but my throbbing headache tells me we had a blast." Without interruption, Carrie collapsed against the refrigerator, barely holding herself up as the tears streamed down.

"Oh, shit Carrie, are you ok? You're going to be fine girl, don't start crying." Jasmine quickly put down the apple pie she just removed from the oven and rushed over to embrace Carrie.

"No, no, no, I'm releasing tears of gratitude. Y'all have no idea; I was going crazy in this house. Literally losing it! I just needed a dose of y'all. At some point I forgot who I was. Being the perfect mommy and wife doesn't mean I can't have fun, too. And ya right Ken, I'm gonna make an appointment with my doctor to be sure all is well with my mind. I need to be proactive about my mental health. Thank ya, thank ya, thank ya!"

Grabbing a box of Kleenex from the guest restroom, I hurried back toward Carrie and dabbed the tears away from her red eyes. "It's our pleasure, girl. Yes, please make sure you take your mental health seriously. We don't need you suffering in silence when there are resources available to help you."

"Oh yeah, you know I'm big on mental health. My monthly meetings with my psychologist are one of my greatest investments. He also incorporates Chinese Medicine techniques that he practiced in his country. Not only can he make my body quiver—" Jasmine quickly buried her head in Carrie's plush bathrobe, trying to hide her embarrassment and cover her ears from our questions.

Carrie and I looked at each other as we both covered our mouths and shouted in unison, "You slept with your psychologist!"

Jasmine started walking toward the guest bedroom to gather her belongings as Carrie and I scurried behind her, eager for more details.

"Look, let's table the details of *my* therapy sessions for our next night of cocktails and conversation. Also, when Miles gets home, let him know we apologize for any evidence he might unearth from our drunken escapade."

Carrie playfully hit Jas on the butt with the belt of her robe. "I love how ya try to dismiss talking about ya salacious sessions with Mr. Psychologist. We can table it, but I won't forget! And, yeah, I called Miles when I woke up and gave him the warning. All he did was laugh."

Hoping to change the subject for good, Jasmine interjected without pause. "Speaking of forgetting, I can't remember *everything* from last night. But Girl, I do remember prank calling my ex Darian and telling him I was pregnant with his baby. That fool started panting like a dog." Jasmine held her chest and started panting as she fell back on the guest bed laughing.

"Are you serious? You do know he's engaged now? That was wrong, Jasmine. Not funny at all." I shook my head at Jasmine as I reached for my phone to find Carvin had texted me several naughty love messages during the night.

Jasmine looked me up and down as she put the last of her items in her overnight bag. "Whatever Ms. Holier than thou. Darian will be *just* fine. If he wasn't a cheating bastard, he wouldn't be concerned about me being pregnant!"

To diffuse the swelling tension, Carrie grabbed our hands and held them against her chest. "Well, at least ya remember something. I honestly don't rememba a thang except that I woke up with a lighta heart. Oh, and a home smelling like Pine Sol and southern comfort food. Thank ya again, ladies."

"Of course, that's what friends are for. To see you sinking and not throw out our life vest of love and support would be an abomination to our friendship. You know crazy Jasmine and I love you, girl." I gave Jas a side eye and a grin to remind her I wasn't done interrogating her about dismissing me for her date.

"I love y'all, too! Thanks for helping me remember who I am."

We hugged and released another round of tears before heading our separate ways, confident that our intervention was a success.

It had been over a week since my weekend retreat with the girls. I promised to dedicate phone, and prayer time on my evening commutes home to Carrie. As I put my briefcase on the back seat and climbed across the passenger seat to the driver side, the vibrating cell phone in my blazer pocket startled me. I pulled it out to find Carrie calling.

"Hey, girl, hold on. I need to get settled in my car. I'm going to call you back once I get on the road."

"Okay, cool. If ya would get a new car and stop driving that piece of junk this wouldn't be an issue," Carrie sarcastically shot back.

"Ha ha! Just let me call you back, smarty pants."

"Please call me back. This is really, *really* important."

"Okay, bye."

"Bye."

Once I got out of the parking garage and on I-45S freeway, I attempted to call Carrie only to find my phone vibrating with her name scrolling across the screen.

"Umm, I thought I said I would call you right back. Is everything okay?"

"I need ya to pull ova and park ya car real quick. This is gonna need ya full attention."

Drowning in a sea of Houston traffic, just the idea of trying to get on the shoulder seemed exhausting. "Clearly you don't realize I'm chilling in Houston's largest parking lot… I-45S. So, what's going on? Are you okay, Carrie?"

"Yes, yes, I'm fine. I promise. Now pull ova," Carrie barked.

All I could do was shake my head. Apparently, my dear friend was hearing impaired. "I can't! I'm in a gridlock on the freeway. Just tell me, Carrie. You're making me nervous. What's going on?"

"Okay, well. Hmmm. Well, afta our great weekend and a couple of sessions with my therapist, I discovered a major factor contributing to my stress was cleaning the house. Afta talking to Miles, he agreed to have a housekeepa come twice a month to clean and help with cooking. Truly the best decision we eva made. Yesterday, while the housekeepa was here, she came across a positive pregnancy test."

"Shut up, girl! I'm excited, but are you all ready for this? You're just getting back into your groove and—"

"Ken, slow down, sista girl. Ya getting way ahead of ya'self. Ya best believe Baby Jack is going to be an only child for *several* more years. But he might have a god sista on the way…" I could sense Carrie smiling on the opposite end.

"Okay, I'm not following…"

Finally, traffic was starting to loosen up, allowing me to release my hands from the steering wheel and ease my foot off the brakes.

"I thought about when y'all were here last weekend and I vaguely rememba one of us taking a pregnancy test, but I couldn't rememba who. Afraid that it was me, I took five pregnancy tests and they were *all* negative. Praise God! I was about to call Jas, but I looked on the back of the stick and saw KMJ scribbled on the back. That's when it all came back to me. Ken, it's you!"

Slamming my foot on the brakes, I jerked forward, coming inches to hitting the car in front of me. My leftover coffee from this morning flew out of my cup holder, painting my pedicured toes café mocha.

"Girl, me and what?"

"Y.O.U. and pregnant…"

"Who is pregnant?"

"You are pregnant!"

"Wait, you mean you are pregnant!"

"Uh no, girl you are."

"Me? Wait… What! Pregnant by whom?" I pulled the phone away from my face and grimaced at the receiver as if the device itself had offended me.

"Really, girl?" Carrie sighed.

"Awww hell no!"

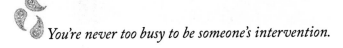 *You should never take a mental health crisis lightly or overlook it when you see signs in those close to you. You just might be the motivation they need to pursue professional attention.*

You're never too busy to be someone's intervention.

There is strength and healing in remembering who you are. Remind yourself daily.

Eighteen

Carvin

f only I had known my real mom. If only my real pops was more than a sperm donor. If only my birth parents had married and decided to raise me in a household that celebrated holidays and birthdays. I've imagined my Pops accompanying me to all my sports practices and championships, coaching me to greatness along the way. My mom would have embodied the characteristics of Claire Huxtable; strong, refined, loving, and graceful. Infatuated by the idea of Claire, I associated that character to my birth mom, oftentimes referring to her as Claire Huxtable. Fictional or not, an image of how she *might* have existed gave my daydreams more life. Our home would be adorned with her loving touch and the kitchen kissed by her lavish meals. I envisioned them being educated and instilling the same values in me. Man, I wanted that so bad. Too bad my fairytale was erased by a contrasting reality.

The moment I escaped Claire's womb my hope for a family began its slow death. For reasons I will never know, she decided to give me away to the Alexanders, a couple who appeared to have the American Dream, but was plagued by the dysfunction of adultery and domestic violence. My prayers for Claire to save me were relentless, but she never came. I guess God had other plans that didn't include answering my prayers. For that reason, I resented Him throughout my early childhood and despised Claire.

Over the years, I've made multiple attempts to locate my birth parents. My adoptive parents did what they could to afford me the best life and education, but their screwed-up marriage and inability to express love carved a painful void in my heart. This further fueled both my anger toward Claire and this insatiable drive to meet her. So, I prayed, and God remained silent. Sadly, I wasn't surprised. Since my adoption was closed, my inquiries were futile. The only positive was I made contacts with several agencies that I hoped would aid in one-day reuniting Ken and her son. Given my track record with the Almighty, I wasn't too optimistic.

Since Ken revealed her adoption, I slowly started to forgive Claire; choosing to believe she gave me away to save me, not abandon me. But, I've also been haunted by images of Ken's son. Knowing the woman I'm about to marry has a son out there who needs her love aggravated my spirit. He deserved to meet his Claire. Although I assured Ken I would be satisfied without a child of my own, as the wedding date approached, my desire for a child of my own resurfaced. As much as I tried, I couldn't shake the need.

One Sunday evening, while enjoying dinner at our favorite restaurant, Pappadeaux's, she revealed the adoption was open. As expected, her self-imposed brick wall of amnesia blocked my efforts to pry for more information.

"I believe the last name of the family who adopted him was Thomas. I honestly can't recall," Kendall replied.

"Do you know what city and state they live in? Do you recall their race? Career?" I leaned back in my seat and watched as she chased the last of her crawfish étouffée down with Merlot.

Making all attempts not to make eye contact, her words tried to make their way around the food and wine. "Maybe Florida or Mississippi. Sorry, babe, I don't know. Let's change the subject, please. How is work?"

Realizing this was sore topic of discussion for Ken, I always pulled back and honored her wishes. Yet, I never stopped probing.

So, I did what I did best: researched and reconnected with one of the Agencies that I consulted with in the past. Although the information provided was limited, I was able to share the birthday and birth hospital, along with Kendall's demographic information. To my surprise, a few weeks later I received a call from my contact stating he might have leads on her son.

After one of my Saturday morning games of basketball with the boys, I changed in the gym locker room and rushed to the agency to meet with the social worker.

As I sat down in his office, Mr. Bill wasted no time getting to the point. "Mr. Alexander, we are not one hundred percent certain, but given the information you provided, we believe he might be Ms. Johnson's son."

"Is there any way to confirm?" I blurted out, holding on to what was left of my breath as he proceeded to answer.

"Without additional identifiers from you, such as a last name of the adopting parents, I'm afraid we will have to act on speculation." He took off his glasses and began to wipe the lenses with a coffee stained napkin before continuing. "Mr. Alexander, I'm hopeful he's her son. Our records indicate this is the only adoption of an African American male that occurred on March 6 at Memorial Hospital."

"So, that sounds promising, right?"

"Sure," he responded as he put his glasses back on. All attempts to cleanse away the dirt only made it worse, as he settled for peering at me over the rim. "But it's not as easy as it appears."

"Exactly, that's why I'm here. What are my options?"

The bass in my voice startled Mr. Bill, as he cleared his throat and adjusted his tie without looking me in the eyes. "Since this was an open adoption, all legal rights belong to the adoptive parents. However, the biological parents have the right to request contact with the child via letter. As previously discussed, our agency has encountered more success with reuniting open adoptions."

The tightening of my chest and burning in my eyes forewarned me of the tears that I refused to release. I took a deep breath, nodding as I tried to order my thoughts. "Okay, okay, okay... Well, let's proceed with establishing contact."

My thoughts immediately started to race at the possibility of Kendall meeting her son and the implications it could have on our future. Maybe if she reunited with him she would consider having my child. Maybe if she held her son, heard his voice, and saw that he was well, she would release the guilt and forgive herself, knowing she offered him a better life. Maybe if her son met her and realized how amazing she was, any of his residual pain or feelings of abandonment will dissipate. Maybe, unlike me, he would have the chance to live a life where he doesn't feel like a piece of his soul was ripped away without his consent. This could be an opportunity for them both to find the closure they deserved.

Mr. Bill interrupted my whirlwind of "maybes" as he continued. "I can send the family a letter stating the biological parent desires to initiate contact with the child; *however*, please understand it is the right of the adoptive family to decline or accept the written request. No response is interpreted and logged by our agency as a decline."

"Interesting. Is it possible for you to provide me with their contact information?" I leaned forward to get a better glimpse of the disheveled pile of forms on his desk.

"No!" Mr. Bill barked as he rashly placed his hands over the documents to shield them from my prying eyes. He placed the documents in a semi-orderly pile and leaned back in his chair. "That, Mr. Alexander, would be unlawful and against our policy. Without consent from the adoptive family, only non-identifying information can be provided." Smoothing out his ruffled vest and readjusting his off-centered glasses, he inhaled slowly. "Their identity will remain confidential and protected."

"I see. Is it possible to request receipt confirmation from the post office? I don't believe that was requested when we tried reaching my birth parents." As Mr. Bill stared blankly at me, unaffected by my insistence, I knew I would have to do something drastic to get him to understand the urgency. "Kendall is deathly ill and her dying wish, along with marrying me, is to meet her son. I would like to surprise her prior to the wedding. Otherwise, I'm afraid she will carry this guilt into our marriage and to the grave. I can't have that. Do you understand the gravity of my request, Mr. Bill?"

Mr. Bill slowly nodded as he rested both arms on the desk, staring through eyes glossed over with pity. "Of course, and I'll do all possible to make your dream a reality. The receipt confirmation should not be an issue. However, I will need a signature from Ms. Johnson confirming her consent. Let's review the paperwork and get started." As Mr. Bill stood and struggled to slither his pudgy frame around the mahogany wood desk, his stomach knocked over his bottle of diet Coke, spilling it all over his desk and pants. He abruptly looked at me with dancing eyes through his crooked bifocals.

"Oh, golly gee gosh! I always do this. Excuse me, Mr. Alexander, let me run to the restroom and collect some paper towels. I will be right back."

He waddled to the door in a mad dash and disappeared. As soon as the door closed, I sank into the dingy metal seat with only the buzzing sound of the rotating desk fan to keep me company. Not knowing what else to do, I resorted to something I had not done in a while; I prayed. As much as I hated to lie to Mr. Bill about Kendall being terminally ill, I was desperate. Although she never verbally expressed a desire to connect with him, the guilt Kendall harbored was proof of her need for closure and forgiveness. Unless she confronted this reality, I feared my wish for a child would never manifest.

As the screeching fan circled back around to me, several papers on the desk fluttered excitedly in the air and sashayed to the ground. Disturbed out of my growing misery, I reached down to collect the misplaced documents from the scuffed tile floor. As I stood to return them to their rightful place on the desk, I noticed one with "Confidential" stamped boldly across the top. As I anxiously scanned the form, I glanced back at the door for fear that Mr. Bill would return and find me snooping. My hands started trembling when I realized it not only contained Kendall's information, but also that of a fourteen-year-old African American boy and his adoptive parents. I immediately grabbed my phone, snapped a picture of the document and placed it back on the desk.

Just as I was straightening the pile, Mr. Bill barged through the door, still overcome with embarrassment. I froze in place, with only my head turning to connect with his eyes.

He looked at me. I looked at him. He looked at the pile of forms. He looked back at me. He watched silently as I slowly pulled my hand from their reach and placed my phone back in my pants pocket. His eyes trailed back to mine as he attempted to clear his throat and fix his disheveled appearance.

As he walked toward me and attempted, yet again, to squeeze back behind his desk, my breathing sped up and the hairs on my neck spiked.

It wasn't until Mr. Bill sat back in his seat that I followed suit.

"Mr. Alexander, you and I have worked together in the past on your personal attempts at locating your parents. One thing you should know I will not do is over promise. I will do all that I can on my behalf to attempt contact. Tomorrow, I can send out the standard letter of request with receipt confirmation. Moving forward, the responsibility to respond is placed on the adoptive parents. Once the document is mailed, it turns into a waiting game."

Wait, is he acting as if he didn't just see me break the law?

Feeling as if the office walls were closing in on me and lunch was slowly making its way north, I did what I could to cut the conversation short. "When should I expect to hear from you?"

"Unfortunately, you're likely not to hear back from me until I've received a response, if any, from the adoptive family. However, after one hundred eighty days, if I have not heard anything from the family, as you already know, I will be forced to close the case." He stared at me as if trying to get a confession from my eyes, but I dared not blink or look away.

"Interesting. Well, I certainly understand. How about this, given the wedding is in six weeks, I will give you two weeks. If I don't hear anything, I will have to research other options."

"I see, well, Mr. Alexander, you do what you need to do. At this time, I'm not sure there is anything further I can do. My role is to assist you to the best of my ability, while remaining both compliant and ethical." Again, he looked down at the documents and back at me. He crossed his arms and leaned back into his metal chair.

Eager to leave the heaviness in the room and my guilt behind, I quickly completed the paperwork and stood up. "I will have Kendall review the forms, sign, and drop the completed documents off in the morning." I firmly shook Mr. Bill's hand, thanking him for his continued assistance over the years.

"My pleasure, Mr. Alexander. I wish you all the best on your journey," he stated with a slight grin as he peered at me over his foggy glasses.

After I dashed out of the office building, I stopped at the nearest bench to gather my composure. I thanked God for His divine intervention and saving grace. More importantly, I apologized for lying and asked for forgiveness. Praying in advance over the last act of deception as I substitute my penmanship for Kendall's signature. Out of respect for Mr. Bill, I promised God I would give him two weeks to work a miracle the legal way. If that fails, I would personally send Mr. and Mrs. Earnest a letter requesting their permission for Kendall Marie Johnson to meet her beloved son, Zachary Earnest, Jr. Although not legal, I was desperate.

Dear Lord, please make a way!

Nineteen

"It's a girl!"

While wiping away sweat from my forehead, Carvin leaned over and kissed my limp lips as he whispered, "Baby, we did it! A healthy baby girl."

Painful exhaustion silenced my attempts to speak. Blinking my eyes to regain focus, I looked past Carvin to see two nurses caring for a newborn baby at the other end of my hospital room.

My mom was smiling as she stood on the tips of her toes, trying to steal a glimpse of the wailing infant. She looked at me, hands on her heart. "Aww, Kendall, she's a perfect mix of you and Carvin. My granddaughter is absolutely beautiful!"

Two nurses approached me and asked if I would like to meet my "little princess." Absent of words, I lay motionless as they placed the stranger on my chest. My parents, Kenton, and Carvin stared at me, eager to witness my response to the chocolate brown, straight-haired angel. As I stared into her small, swollen eyes, the walls hiding my heart came crashing down. Tears flowed as I found the strength to say, "Hi, sweetie."

Leaning forward to kiss my daughter, I shuddered as a sea of blackness overshadowed her honey brown eyes. Spitting in my face, she growled through a mouth full of teeth, "I hate you. You abanonded my brother. I hate you! I hate you!"

I looked up at my family; their faces morphed with distorted versions of my son's face, taunting me with growls and grimaces.

Right before Carvin reached forward to choke me, I screamed as I felt an invisible force jerking my shoulder.

"Kendall! Kendall, wake up!"

"I'm sorry! I… I… I…" Startled from my nightmare, I lifted my head from the nest of my arms to find Andy leaning over me with wrinkled brows.

"Kendall, what are you sorry about? What's going on?"

"Oh, gosh." I wiped away the slobber smeared across my cheeks and discreetly attempted to dig the sleep from my eyes. "I'm so sorry, Ms. Williams, somehow I fell asleep and had a nightmare of some sorts. But, I'm fine."

Not satisfied with my response, Andy leaned in closer, eyes peering over her tortoiseshell Christian Dior glasses. "Look, Kendall, if there is something you need to talk about, I'm all ears. I know you all call me Cruella behind my back, but I do have a heart somewhere." She patted the left side of her chest as she stepped back, turning her attention to my laptop screen. Clearing her throat, she looked back at me, her eyes soft and embracing.

As I followed her eyes, I gasped and slammed my laptop shut. "Ms. Williams, I appreciate your concern, but I'm fine. Thank you."

Looking at the clock, I quickly pushed back from my desk, grabbed my purse, and reached to turn off the overhead light. All the while, Andy stood at the entrance of my cubicle, as if waiting for an explanation for the contents displayed on my computer. To get her out of my hair, I decided a lie would be my greatest escape tactic.

"As for that," I tapped on my laptop and then grabbed it, placing it in my briefcase, "that's for a friend who is contemplating other options. She didn't want to research the other options at home; afraid her husband may come across it."

"Hmm, okay." Andy looked at her watch and back at me. Rolling her hazel eyes ever so slightly, itching to interrogate me more, but clearly needing to head to her afternoon meeting, she asked, "Is it safe to assume your friend's personal matters will not interfere with your upcoming project in Eritrea? I have put a lot on the line, Kendall, to support your vision. I hope you honor that appropriately."

"Of course. I can assure you my friend's issue is a *very private, separate* matter."

Andy nodded her head in silence, searching my face for doubt. "Umph. That's good to know. I say this sincerely, Kendall. Please know I'm here for you." She curtly pivoted and sauntered in the direction of her office, her black pleated skirt sweeping the aisle.

As if she remembered a very important detail, she abruptly turned back toward me, waving her hand in my direction. "Ah, your friend. I meant, if your *friend* needs me just let me know. Given I'm a *proud* Pro-Choice advocate, we just might have more in common than she thinks." Putting emphasis on *friend*, she winked before disappearing into her office.

Awkward. Andy always had a way of disturbing my spirit with her intrusive approach. If my mind wasn't so beaten by stress of the new addition, I might have had more energy to tango with her, but not today.

Leaning my head back, I sank into my chair, closing my eyes with a long exhale. Since the revelation of my pregnancy, Guilt's presence had become more invasive and vengeful. Stealing my dreams to taunt me with cryptic visions of my first love or showing up uninvited and refusing to leave. Somehow, it managed to lull me to sleep during lunch, causing me to miss my twelve-week follow-up appointment. Not that it mattered; I had already claimed my course of action. Although, deep, deep, deep down I was secretly hoping Dr. Flan would use his scientific rhetoric and persuade me to choose life.

I took the glitch in my plans as a divine sign to proceed with the promise I made to my sixteen-year-old self. There was *no* way I would bring another child into this world and love it unconditionally. I waived my rights to motherhood when I gave my son away. To even know I was considering this child made my stomach cringe and eyes burn. How selfish of me! Guilt concurred as its warmth crept further up my back, squeezing my shoulders tighter, reminding me of what I don't deserve. As long as Carvin was oblivious to my extra baggage, I would tuck away the pending abortion as a forgotten memory. Guilt grinned.

Now all I needed to do was make an appointment.

 Recognize when guilt or shame misguides your decisions. They are symptoms of unresolved issues that, when unaddressed, can sabotage your joy and peace.

Don't give your past the power to dictate your future.

Twenty

Carvin

Growing up, I was always a loner. After basketball or football practice, hanging out at my place was not an option. My parents offered, but I was too afraid my teammates would be introduced to the dysfunction they called marriage. Between Dad sharing his dick with the PTA mothers and Mom spying around like a pitiful Pink Panther, I just couldn't risk the scar to my reputation.

With my evolving maturity and acceptance to Virginia National University, friendships miraculously evolved. One of them was with my frat brother Miles. While dating Carrie during our junior year, they both decided I would be the perfect match for her sorority sister. Cupid's arrow was not my thing, but after seeing her pictures on Black Planet, I decided to give in to their matchmaking scheme. I definitely wasn't expecting the piercing arrows Ken shot my way. Smooth chocolate skin, intellect, and a biscuit booty were my weaknesses. Blessed with all three: beauty, brains, and a booty like a newly opened can of biscuits, just thinking about my Ken made my mind speak and my dick respond.

Unfortunately, with our decision to abstain from sex until our wedding night, the response of my loins fell on deaf ears. But I was good. With three weeks left until the wedding and my efforts to reunite Kendall with her son starting to produce results, sex was the last thing on my mind.

Following our engagement, I promised Kendall I would be more intentional with my spiritual growth. Attending church more consistently was my first step. On this particular Sunday, I sat next to Kendall as Pastor Paul preached from Ezekiel 37, inspiring the congregation to prophesy to the dry bones in the desert areas of their lives. As I held Kendall's hand, massaging her palm, my mind wandered to her dry bones. During my visit with Mr. Bill, I was first introduced to Zachary on the confidential document. I silently prayed for God to breathe life into the situation. It had been almost a month since my meeting at the agency and I had not heard anything from Mr. Bill. The anxiety behind this door of opportunity possibly closing interrupted my focus during the service. Something had to give, or I feared my future wife would crumble and my dream for a child would be lost.

Sensing my angst, Kendall rubbed my thigh and rested her head on my shoulder. Looking up at me, she smiled and whispered, "Is my Carvin okay?"

Kissing the top of her head, I placed my arm around her shoulders and pulled her closer. "Of course, I'm cool. The message is just speaking to me, that's all. I love you." I turned my attention back to the pulpit, determined to receive the rest of the message.

The boisterous sound of somebody's Verizon wireless chime broke my focus. Irritated, I looked at the congregants around me, hoping my piercing eyes would convince the guilty party to promptly silence their cell phone. One thing that irked me more than people talking loud in the movie theatre was when someone neglected to mute their phone in church.

As I turned to Kendall, my frustration found her glaring back at me. "Turn off your phone, Carvin," she whispered.

I followed her darting eyes toward my phone that had somehow fallen beneath the pew in front of us. While trying to ignore the stares from neighboring members, I discreetly attempted to retrieve it with my left foot. By the time it was within arm's reach, the loud ringing had stopped. After turning it on vibrate, I checked my call history for the name of the idiot calling me. Unfortunately, it was a number I didn't recognize.

"Who was calling you?" Kendall whispered, never once taking her eyes off Pastor Paul.

"Your guess is as good as mine." I showed her the unknown number, before placing my cell in my blazer pocket.

"Mississippi?"

"Huh?" Grabbing her hand and intertwining it in mine, I asked, "What about Mississippi?"

"The number. It's a Mississippi area code," Kendall responded matter-of-factly.

There was no doubt in my mind that the mysterious call was not from a collection agency. One thing I didn't tolerate was paying late on bills and hoarding debt. To my satisfaction and relief, Kendall was just as meticulous.

As the pocket of my blazer vibrated, I rested Ken's hand back on her lap and nodded toward the restroom. Scooting out of the pew, I quickly headed out the exit and grabbed my phone to identify the anonymous caller.

Listening to the voicemail, a delightful, southern accent greeted my ears. *"I believe this to be the mailbox of Mr. Alexander. Hi, sir, my name is Mary Earnest. You contacted us recently regarding our baby boy, Zach. I, um. Well, my husband and I would like to chat. We received your letter regardin' a Ms. Kendall, Zach's birth mother. Please call as soon as ya can. God bless ya sir.*"

The line went silent as I balled my fist up and pumped it into the air. I stepped outside onto the lush church lawn, as my finger made a mad dash toward the call button.

"Good morning, this is Mary Earnest."

I bit my left fist to subdue my excitement. Shaking my hands and shoulders to settle my nerves, I exhaled deeply before responding. "Hello, Mrs. Earnest, this is Carvin Alexander, Kendall Marie Johnson's fiancé. I was—"

"Oh, yes! Charlie, hurry to the phone. It's Mr. Alexander." The phone was flooded with static as I heard what I assumed was Charlie grabbing the other phone.

"I'm sorry, Mr. Alexander, my husband and I both would like to speak with you. You see, we got your letter and are delighted—"

She was immediately drowned out by Mr. Earnest's deep, southern drawl.

"Howdy, Carvin, my sweetheart and I thank you for returnin' our call. We're quite delighted you reached out to us regardin' our son. I'll admit we're curious as to why. In the letter you mentioned Ms. Kendall being under the weather?"

I stood in silence, staring at the cross adorning the apex of our church building. To be a lie away from Kendall meeting her son was such sweet temptation. Before I could speak, Pastor Paul's words interrupted my scheme, "*To truly see a miracle happen, you have to give your dry bones over to God and allow Him to breathe into them.*"

"About the illness…" I nervously inhaled. "Kendall is not necessarily sick…yet. To be honest, I'm afraid the guilt and anguish behind giving her son away might manifest itself as a chronic illness if she doesn't forgive herself soon." I poured out the truth in one breath, clenching my fists in anticipation of their response.

The phone fell silent for a few moments as the heat from the July sun teased my forehead. As I opened my mouth to explain further, Mrs. Earnest interrupted.

"Okay, so you're sayin' the letter was a lie? Hmm, well Mr. Alexander, that doesn't fare well with us. Our willingness to even entertain your request was because we didn't want our son to resent us. To forbid him the opportunity of meeting his birth mother before she died was—" Sniffling and soft whimpers replaced her words as they trailed off.

I heard Mr. Earnest urging his wife to calm down as he took over the conversation. "What my wife is trying to say is that we don't appreciate you misleading us. Not one bit!"

"Mr. Earnest, I understand and truly apologize for—"

"I would have to disagree. My wife and I have pondered for many nights over making this call and to find out you were a con artist all along… Well, sir, that's a devil shame," Mr. Earnest snapped, without a pause.

As much as I wanted to beg and even demand their cooperation, I trusted God would give these dry bones life. "You're right about that, but wrong about my apology being disingenuous. I'm by no means a villain, nor do I intend to intrude without your permission. If you choose not to entertain my request…I, uh… well, I promise to honor that."

Once again, the silence was stifling, but this time it was apparent Mr. and Mrs. Earnest had covered the phone with their hands. Their muffled discussion could be heard, but not interpreted. The whispers stopped and Mrs. Earnest continued.

"We are aware of your character, Mr. Alexander. My husband is a Sheriff, so he diligently reviewed you and Ms. Kendall's background before we called. In addition, we contacted Mr. Bill White, given we had received the letter of inquiry from his agency shortly before yours arrived. He was quite perturbed and asked if we wanted to file a formal grievance against you. We assured him that wasn't necessary...yet. That is subject to change."

The growing knot in my throat, rapid beat in my chest, and unforgiving heat from the sun wouldn't allow me to respond. *Lord, what have I gotten myself into? These dry bones are turning into ash. For once God, please answer my prayer and start breathing in them... Like now.*

"Interestingly enough," Mrs. Earnest continued, "Zach recently started askin' about his birth folks. Given we're white and he is Black, we expected this time would come and have always prayed that God would give us wisdom on what to do. The day after he first asked, the letter from the agency arrived. Charlie and I prayed and fasted for two weeks, seeking God for His direction. On the final day of our fast, guess what happened?"

Unsure, I stuttered, "Um, God answered?"

Mr. and Mrs. Earnest gently chuckled in unison. "Don't sound so unsure of His faithfulness," Mrs. Earnest said. "Of course, He answered. God always answers. The *when* and *how* is what we tend to lose our faith around. In this case, He answered in a miraculous way. Our Zach asked us a second time about his birth parents. Yet, the miracle is in the arrival of your letter. On the *exact same day!*"

"My wife and I took your letter to be God's answer. So, I did my research on you and Ms. Kendall. Mr. Alexander, we want Zach to meet Ms. Kendall out of obedience to God. This has nothing to do with you or us. We are actually still uncomfortable with the idea."

"Humph, and with your lies, I'm tempted to be disobedient, but I love God too much. Do understand that I will not put my baby boy in danger for you, my husband, or anyone else!"

After hearing the harshness in Mrs. Earnest's tone, I glanced at the cross as I silently thanked God for His mercy and grace.

Again, there was whispering in the background before Mr. Earnest said, "Our apologies, Mr. Alexander. I hope you can understand my sweet Claire's disappointment. Now I'm a little more patient because I was adopted and made attempts to find my birth parents. Years after my adoptive parents died, I discovered my birth mom tried to contact me when I was around our boy's age, but my adoptive parents refused. We don't want that to be the case with our Zach."

Wait, Claire. Who is Claire? Mom? "I'm sorry, but who is Claire?"

"Oh, my apologies for the confusion Mr. Alexander. Mary Claire Earnest is my wife. Family and friends call her by her middle name, Claire."

Hold up! Had God just answered my prayer in the most unimaginable way? Throughout my childhood, I constantly prayed for "Claire" to find and rescue me. Who knew the "Claire" I was praying for would show up almost twenty years later to save both me and my future wife. For the next fifteen minutes or so, I shared additional apologies, my story of being adopted, and the significance of Claire's name. We also discussed how to coordinate the initial meeting between Kendall and Zach. It turned out Mr. and Mrs. Earnest would be in Houston for a church conference the week of our wedding and agreed to schedule a meet and greet during that time. However, under one condition. They requested a separate meeting with Kendall and their lawyer a few days beforehand. Depending on the outcome of the meeting, they would decide if it was appropriate to continue with the introduction.

God always answers. Don't allow your faith to be shaken because you don't know when or how He will answer. Trust Him. When He does answer, it will be at the right time and in the right way.

God can only work with what you surrender to Him. Let it go and give "it" to God. Watch Him work!

Twenty-One

"Where are you?" Carvin blurted through the phone, void of a greeting.

"Uh, well, hello to you, too," I snapped back while cutting through I-10 traffic.

"A'ight, enough with the antics, Kendall. Where are you at?"

"Minding mine! Call me back after you've taken Phone Etiquette 101."

Patience wearing thin, Carvin let out a deep moan. "Kendall, is there something you need to tell me?"

Uh, yeah, I'm headed to the abortion clinic to save myself some agony was what I wanted to say, but I decided on a simple, "No, why?"

"Okay, I see how this is going to go. You're pregnant, Ken. You're pregnant and didn't even *think* of telling me, that's what!"

"Excuse me? What are you talking about?" *Ah crap, how in the hell did he find out?* The last distraction I needed right now was Carvin trying to drown me in more guilt and condemnation. Unfortunately, for him, I had made up my mind and scheduled the appointment; I did not intend to renege on the promise I made to my sixteen-year-old self.

"Ha, okay. I see we're on a three-way call with amnesia. Well, let me bring you both up to speed. While cleaning out your car this morning, I came across some papers in your glove compartment..."

Carvin's words trailed off as he waited for me to confess. I deferred my comments.

"So, you still have no idea what I'm talking about, huh? Okay, so explain the pamphlet with instructions on how to prepare the night before for an abortion, and a document confirming your scheduled... Wait, are we really going to play this game, Kendall?"

"First off, why were you snooping through my glove compartment? Explain that! No one asked you to clean out my car. The way I keep my car is *my business!*" I took a deep breath, hoping my attempts to displace blame would prove successful. One exit from the clinic and already several minutes late for my appointment, my only option was to get Carvin off the phone, and quick.

"Are you kidding me, Kendall? You're about to go commit murder. Yes, murder, and you're focused on a damn dashboard!" Carvin seethed through gritted teeth. In the background, I could hear a lot of commotion followed by him slamming what sounded like his car door. "Kendall Marie, where are you at?"

"Carvin, I'm not going to get into an argument with you right now. I'll call you later—"

"Hell nah, we're talking right now. Are you at the clinic? Never mind, don't answer. I'm on my way there now. We are not having an abortion, Kendall!"

"Listen, Carvin, this is not about you. *I* am the one carrying the baby. *I* am the woman in this equation! It is *my* constitutional right to decide on the life of this child, *not* you. *My* body, *my* health, *my* future, and *my* career will be impacted the most. Me, Carvin, me!" I cried out. "*You* can walk away at any time, choose not to be present and get a pass. *I* don't have that luxury as a woman. *I* abandoned one son already. I did that! I do not have room in my heart to care for another child. My heart is somewhere outside of me trying to find him! I'm so sorry, but—" As my voice breaks, my hands begin to shake and Guilt arrives to comfort me.

"But what, Kendall? You don't have to be sorry. Just don't do it! Let go of the guilt, Kendall! All this guilt is going to kill you. Let it go. Look, I will take care of the baby. You know I will. Better yet, you can stop working and I will carry the household. Just please, Ken, please..." He sniffled and struggled to clear his throat as his voice trembled on, "... just please don't kill my dream, our legacy. Please, babe. Please let me give my child what my parents never gave me," he pleaded as the phone fell silent.

As I approached the clinic, the raucous chanting of several pro-life advocates parading outside the complex disturbed our silence. Signs showing mutilated fetuses and Bible references marched in sequence with the protesters. Relief set in when the traffic light turned red.

"Look, Carvin, I need to go. Clearly, you just don't get it. You. Don't. Get. It! I will *hate* myself and resent you for making me break my promise. I can't. I just can't." We continued to argue back and forth. Luckily, there was no traffic behind me, so I was able to sit briefly at the light while our words collided. Carvin pleaded for me to trust him with the life of our unborn child, as I remained settled in my decision.

Before I could finish my final argument, Carvin's desperation interrupted my point. "Baby, when will you realize I am not your enemy? Can you just wait until I arrive? Please. I'm less than ten minutes away. I need you to do this for me...for us. To hell with what Roe vs. Wade says, as the father, I have the right to what's half of me. Am I at least worth you waiting a few minutes to discuss this together? Damn!"

My silence replied to his question, as I was fixated on the many protestors marching to my left and right. One stole my attention. He was a strikingly handsome teenaged boy, looked to be no older than sixteen. Adorned in a red cap worn backward, black skinny jeans, a gray hoodie, and red Chucks. He shouted passionately at the passing traffic, "Choose life, trust Christ! Choose life, trust Christ." Before I could turn away and answer Carvin's lingering question, our eyes locked. The tall, slender teenager smiled at me while pointing to his sign that read: *Abortion almost stole my life, but she chose adoption. I don't know her, but my future thanks her.*

For the next few moments, my tear-drenched eyes darted between the young boy and the sign. When our eyes met again, my heart whispered what my quivering lips could not, "Choose life, trust Christ."

My breathing became erratic as I struggled to catch my breath between sobs. *Had I given my son the best by simply gifting him life?*

My heart gently whispered, *Yes.*

But, I abandoned him, right?

My heart whispered, *No, sweetheart, you gifted him life.*

But, how can I love another child when my son is out there motherless?

With the same love you showed when you gifted him away. You have all the love you need. Honor him by loving another. Forgive yourself. My heart pleaded.

My heart rhythm relaxed as a weightless force slowly teased away the heaviness surrounding me. Although uncomfortable at first, I gradually gave Forgiveness permission to baptize me in the warmth of its love.

Aware of my changing heart, the sheet of Guilt slithered up my backside to the nape of my neck, snuggling against my ear as it tried to counter Forgiveness with images of my abandoning my son. However, Guilt no longer felt like velvet, but brittle and abrasive. Yet, strange enough, still inviting.

Before I could succumb to the embrace that was once so comfortable to me, his eyes snatched mine again. He held my gaze and smiled as he pointed to his sign. In a matter of seconds, Guilt began to loosen its grip as Forgiveness massaged my heart. My trembling hands attempted to wipe away the tears painting my lips as I screamed, "Oh, God, please release me from this guilt. Forgive me and show me how to forgive myself!"

As guilt begrudgingly whisked away, I felt my breathing calm and my thoughts flat line. It was as if I had an aha! moment for the first time in my adult life. No longer would I willingly be a slave to self-pity and guilt. As the tenderness of Forgiveness descended upon me, I smiled back at the young kid, nodding my head in acceptance. Self-forgiveness was a choice I had finally decided to start embracing.

The faint sound of Carvin screaming my name from the passenger side floor abruptly broke our gaze. My eyes followed his muffled rant and found my cell phone had strangely fallen to the floor. Eager to share my epiphany, I briefly took my eyes off the road and reached down to grab my phone. As I placed the receiver to my right ear, smiling with anticipation, I accidentally slammed my foot on the gas pedal and sped into oncoming traffic. I heard Carvin saying, "Let's please pray together, baby," before all went silent.

The most important person to forgive is you. As you extend compassion and forgiveness to yourself, you give yourself permission to do the same for others.

Forgiveness and Guilt are a choice. Which will you choose?

In order for true love and intimacy to thrive, you must realize your significant other is NOT your enemy. Love is a partnership, not a war.

Twenty-Two

Carvin

"Kendall! Kendall! I hear you in the background. Please talk to me... Let's please pray together, baby. Let God make the final decision. Hello? Hello? Kendall!"

Pressing my foot on the gas pedal, I maneuvered through I-10 traffic, almost missing my exit. Choking the steering wheel with my clenched palms, I let out an exasperated "Damn it!" I couldn't believe Kendall would hang up on me right after asking her to pray.

To avoid passing my exit, I swerved my Benz Coupe in front of an F150 truck, almost causing a collision. I raised my right hand of truce to the truck driver behind me only for him to curse me with his blaring horn. As I sped through the red light and made a sharp right, I attempted to call Kendall again, only to get her voicemail. Not only did she hang up on me, she had the audacity to ignore my calls. Unable to contain my frustration, I punched my right fist against the steering wheel, accidentally blowing the horn as I further anchored my foot on the gas pedal. Reaching her before the doctor did was my goal.

As I looked in my rearview mirror, the dancing lights of an ambulance headed in my direction further agitated my annoyance. As much as I appreciated our emergency response teams' sense of urgency, having to pull over and let them rush by was not my preference. Although tempted to speed up in front of them, my Good Samaritan conscience wouldn't allow me to do so. As the shrieking sirens dashed ahead of me, I took advantage of the opportunity and followed suit.

Engaging the right turn signal to announce the turn before my final destination, I was intrigued by the EMS making an abrupt turn in the same direction. Soon after we turned, I noticed several police cars and fire trucks about five hundred feet ahead, right outside the clinic. Attempting to avoid the frenzy, I made another quick right and parked behind the complex.

Once parked, I jumped out of the car and phoned Kendall again, only for the sweet sound of her voicemail to serenade me. My stomach twisted and my heart throbbed as I stared at the gray, lifeless metal door in front of me. Taking a deep breath, I opened it. A complete contrast to the morbid exterior, soft splashes of pink and yellow accessories, modern décor, and soft music offered a more welcoming interior. The receptionist at the back entrance slid the glass partition window to the side and ushered me in with her greeting. "Hi, sir, did you have an appointment?"

"Uh, yeah, um, Kendall Marie Johnson. I'm meeting my fiancée, Kendall, here for a four-thirty appointment." Rubbing my hands together to dry off some of the sweat, I walked up to the counter and grabbed a complimentary water bottle.

"Hmm, I'm sorry, sir. It appears Ms. Johnson was a no-show for her appointment. She did call to say she was running late, but that was close to an hour ago." The young receptionist's smiling eyes stared back at me.

"Strange. I just spoke with her and she was out front. Do you mind if I wait here for a moment?" I turned to find a nice pink and yellow floral print armchair, and took a seat.

"Unfortunately, we closed at five o'clock. My apologies." She proceeded to place the closed sign on the counter outside the partition. "I thought I locked the back door, but with the crazy car accident outside, I've been a little distracted."

"Oh, my bad, ma'am. I completely lost track of time." I glimpsed at my watch. It was five-fifteen. As I slowly rose and headed back the way I entered, I abruptly turned back toward the receptionist. Brows furrowed, left hand rubbing my forehead, and eyes closed, I took a deep breath before asking, "So, does this mean she didn't have an abortion?" Holding my breath hostage, I opened my eyes to find blue eyes of pity staring back at me.

"Due to patient confidentiality, I cannot discuss that matter with you. However, the process of elimination speaks volumes. I'm sorry, sir."

I knelt and collapsed my head into my open palms as I let out a loud exhale of relief. Standing back up, I fist pumped the air and returned my attention to the now confused woman. "Nah, don't be sorry! Thank you, Lord! Whoa!" Clapping, I skipped back toward the back entrance.

"Sir, there's a possibility Ms. Johnson parked out front and when she came to our doors found them locked. There are still several cars blocked due to the accident. She could be out there. If you want, you can exit through the front."

"Sure, why not," I chimed.

Just knowing I had an opportunity to save my child's life gave me peace. We were not getting an abortion; I just had to find a way to convince Kendall. I eagerly followed the receptionist through the back lobby toward the front of the clinic. As I exited through the front door, the loud sounds of sirens and gasps from onlookers violated my euphoria. Burnt rubber, gasoline, and random comments from spectators stifled the air.

"How terrible!"

"I saw the whole thing! Poor lady went right through the windshield!"

"She was waiting to turn at the light and I saw her reach down for something. Next thing I know, her car just sped head-on into traffic!"

"Was she headed to the clinic?"

"God bless her soul!"

"Do you think it was suicide?"

"My God, I hope she wasn't pregnant!"

I quickly scanned the parking lot for Kendall's car, yet none belonged to her. *Did she decide to leave? Maybe she parked in the back to avoid the crazy scene.* My greatest hope was that she changed her mind. *But, why wouldn't she answer my calls? Kendall loves to pray, so why would she hang up on me when I asked her to pray?* It just didn't add up.

Finally accepting she wasn't at the clinic, I leaned up against the brick building and tried her again. As I glanced at my phone, I saw a recent missed call from Kendall. Before hitting send, I looked toward Heaven and asked God for His strength, mercy, and patience. I spent a few moments rehearsing how I was going to approach her, choosing to be gentle and listen first. *Lord, give me strength.*

The phone rang four to five times before she answered. Expecting to hear Kendall, instead I heard what sounded like loud sirens and several background voices, similar to the scene in front of me.

Is she here? My heart slammed against my chest as I took several steps toward the crowd, frantically searching the perimeter for her. "Hello, Kendall? Are you there? Can you hear me, baby?"

"Hello," responded a deep, male's voice, "May I please ask who I'm speaking to?"

I removed the phone from my ear to check the caller ID. "Who am I? The question is *who* are you? This is my fiancée's phone. *Who* are you and *why* are you answering?"

"Hello, sir, this is Officer Rick Neil. I called and left you a message about five minutes ago regarding Ms. Kendall Johnson. I'm sorry, but she was in a serious accident and has suffered life-threatening injuries..."

As his words trailed off, all I heard was "accident" and "life-threatening" before my eyes landed on her mangled car, less than two-hundred feet away from me. I stood paralyzed, my feet too heavy to move, my thoughts too rapid to think. My legs buckled under the weight of the scene and I fell to my knees. Two women rushed to my aid and yelled for help. Within seconds, three men interlocked their arms around me and ushered my limp body to a nearby bench.

"Sir, are you okay? Sir? Sir?"

Blinking, trying to refocus, I found the strength to whisper, "Kendall, she is my fiancée. Accident? She is pregnant! Our baby! No!" Tears exploded forth as I screamed, "Where is she? Where is Kendall?"

This had to be a nightmare. With opened palms, I started pounding myself on the head to end the dream, but the scenery never changed. I looked up to find several concerned strangers lingering over me. As I attempted to stand up and force my trembling body through the crowd, I started yelling out Kendall's name and the only responses were stares of sadness.

I followed the sound of a familiar voice shouting my name and found Kendall's mother waving by the scene of the accident. Biting my bottom lip and clenching my fists to try to redirect the pain, I hastened toward her, allowing her wilted, convulsing frame to fall into mine. Several officers guided us toward a less populated area as they proceed to recreate the tragedy.

When Mrs. Johnson asked about Kendall's prognosis, the officers glanced at each other, and then back at us. One officer removed his shades to wipe his reddened eyes before breaking the silence. "Unfortunately, from our understanding, it doesn't look good, Mrs. Johnson."

"I need to see Kendall. Let me see her please, please. I need to see her and protect her. She is pregnant! No, no, no!" Yelling her name through tears, I attempted to barge past the officers, but they exerted their joint strength, refusing to allow me to go in the direction of the scene.

"I'm very sorry, sir. Officer Neil can escort you both to the hospital now."

Today

So, here I am today, anchored to a hospital bed and adorned with medical equipment. The only bling I have is the sporadic light from my vital signs machine. Mom, Dad, and Jasmine have proven to be my most faithful supporters, with Mom remaining at bedside most days. However, what I have come to value most are the visits from Dad. Every morning, rain or shine, he has his first cup of coffee at my bedside. Mom often uses this time to go shower and eat breakfast, allowing Dad and me this time alone. During these intimate mornings, he recounts funny childhood stories, brings me up-to-date on Kenton's most recent mission trip to the Philippines, or shares his disappointment with the political climate and the injustices of police brutality. When in his presence, the confinements of my current situation lift as I get lost in his love and current events. However, as soon as my guests leave, Guilt eagerly brings me back to reality. Specifically, reminding me of Carvin's absence.

The last time I heard his voice it shivered with disdain and fatigue. Carvin was hurting and the thought of what he believed I was going to do was the cause of it. Even more hurtful was that I lost our child in the process of trying to give it life. Unfortunately, he would never know.

As the days pass, I feel the presence of death looming closer. To be honest, this is frightening. Just yesterday, the Cardiopulmonary Resuscitation team was at my bedside because my heart stopped beating. The idea of approaching the unknown is eerie. As much as I try to suppress the thoughts, I find myself obsessed with Guilt and the grave possibility of dying with regrets. Still having a spiritual chest of gems I have yet to discover. At thirty, there is a mountain of life for me still to climb: marry Carvin, document poverty overseas, buy a home, go sky diving, write a book, ride a camel, learn a second language, and have another baby. The bucket list is infinite. Yet, the most heart wrenching reality is dying without my son ever knowing my love for him. That is unfathomable.

Wait. Is that the door?

With his familiar Egyptian musk scent infusing the air, it reaches me before words.

Oh, my gosh, my Carvin is back.

"Hi, Ken. I, um. Where do I even start? I just, I needed some time to figure things out." Moments of silence intrude as I hear him pull up a chair next to me. Leaning in, he uses the back of his hand to caress my cheek. He appears to be studying my face for any signs of life. So close, I can smell the remnants of Listerine on his breath. "I started back seeing my therapist from childhood to help me process my pain. Not only was I angry regarding the death of our child and your injuries, but another facet of my hurt evolved from a more selfish place."

If only he knew. I could care less about the past. His being here, right now, is all that matters. I quiet my thoughts as he continues.

"Um, I found Zachary. Your son, Kendall. I found him. I found your son. The day of the accident I was planning for you to meet his adoptive parents. That's one of the reasons why I washed your car that day, I wanted everything about you to perfect. And, because I love you". Carvin pauses to clear his throat and reposition himself, grabbing both my hands. "But yeah. Man, I was so excited Ken! I hoped by meeting him you would let go of the guilt and open yourself up to having a child with me."

Wait... What? Zachary. You found my son! His name is Zachary. Oh. My. God. Oh, my God! Please, don't say any more, Carvin. If this is a joke to get back at me, please don't... I can't handle it, Carvin.

"They wanted to meet you first. But, life happened. After your accident, I met with them later that week and..."

And, what?

I feel my chest compressing upon itself as I try to brace myself for what I believe he might say next. The beeps from the respirator appear to be taunting me as they speed up and merge as my heart struggles to respond. Racing, my thoughts try to keep my brain alive.

I'm dying, it's over! Oh no, God, I'm dying! Oh, Lord, help me, I'm—

"Kendall, I met Zachary... I met your son. Man, that little dude is nothing short of amazing!"

Wait. What?

Immediately, I snap out of my nightmare as I hear Carvin's last words.

Come again...

Carvin chuckles to himself as I hear him lean back in his seat. I imagine him with his hands interlocked behind his head as he stares at the ceiling, reminiscing. "And his parents have taken excellent care of him. You may not know it, but some late nights I would hear you praying for him and his adoptive parents, that they would love and adore him. God listened and honored you. Baby, you would be proud. And wait, this is crazy. Would you believe his birth mom's name is Claire? Claire!" The chair creaks as it responds to Carvin's expressed excitement. "*Man*, I was blown away baby. All these years I've been praying to meet this make-believe projection of my mom named Claire, and she came. I mean, she is not *my* mom, but his mom and… You get what I'm trying to say. God does answer prayers, baby. He really does. My answer came for you. Man, my God!"

Wow! Please share, babe. Please tell me about my first love.

"I laugh because he not only looks like you, but dude is just as stubborn. And, like you, he has a heart of gold. Tall as hell and loves basketball. He is everything about you that is good." Carvin lets out a cracked exhale, shuffling uncomfortably in the chair. "Zach is loving and smart like you, and kinda corny like you, too." Carvin's laugh is interrupted by the creaking of my hospital room door.

The soft voice of Nurse Renee extends an apology for intruding before informing Carvin that some visitors named Mr. and Mrs. Earnest would like to visit. Carvin gives her permission to invite them up, stating he would meet them in the hallway first. Nurse Renee expresses understanding, and gently closes the door.

Without invitation, my thoughts immediately race again, as Carvin proceeds to say that Mr. and Mrs. Earnest are Zachary's parents. He explains how Zachary personally requested to meet me, and his parents agreed. My parents were thrilled to meet Zachary yesterday, and agreed with him meeting me before he heads back to Mississippi tonight.

"Kendall, I know you can't hear me. At this point, I don't even know if you're still in there. I love you, baby. Everything about you brings me joy. Please know that. And, I want to believe God has allowed you to hang on for this moment. The moment you finally get to meet your son. Zachary—" Another knock at the door interrupts Carvin "That's him. He is here. Zachary is here to meet you."

Carvin kisses both my hands and lips before excusing himself to step out into the hallway, leaving me alone with my anxious thoughts.

Oh, my gosh! Zach is here. My first love is here and he is about to see me like this. No, Carvin, not like this, Carvin, please not like this. Oh my, oh my, oh my… He is going to hate me. My poor baby is going to have so many questions that I will not be able to answer. Lord, God, please intervene. I would love to see him, hold him, and reassure him my love never left or faltered, but not like this-

My thoughts are arrested mid-sentence as the door slowly squeaks open and Carvin whispers to his new companion. "It's okay, Zach. I want you to meet her." After a few moments of coaxing, Carvin's heavy steps head in my direction, as softer, more hesitant steps follow. I shudder, as I perceive my first love moving closer to me. My anxiety drowns out all other noise as I focus on each of his steps. With my keen sense of hearing, I notice Carvin's breathing speed up, while Zach's slows to almost nothing.

"Hey lil-man, it's okay. You can breathe. This is Kendall Marie Johnson, your birth mother. You can touch her." After some shuffling around, the youthful scent of deodorant and physical activity dilutes the smell of Carvin's signature cologne. He is standing next to me.

"Um, is she alive, Mr. Carvin? Can she hear me?"

His voice is heavenly. Slightly raspy with puberty fighting to erase any traces of his high-pitched boyhood. Through the darkness of my vision, I can sense Carvin smile as he steps closer to respond.

"Yeah, she is very much alive. And, I like to believe she can hear us." Carvin goes on to educate Zach on the various medical equipment keeping me alive. At this moment, my body stiffens with emotion and II believe my ears tingle from the excitement of having the two men I love most standing by my side. The desire to cry is so painful to my spirit. The wish to be able to express my emotion gnaws at my heart.

"Mr. Carvin, can I, um. Is it okay if I touch her hand? I mean, I won't hurt her... *Will I?*"

"Nah, of course not. Go ahead. She would love that."

Before I feel the softness of his hand, the warmth of his approach causes my spirit to shiver.

Oh, my gosh! Is this really happening, Lord? Is my son actually touching me?

I feel a lump invade my throat, although uncertain if it is a figment of my imagination. The aching desire to respond emotionally is agonizing.

"It's okay, Zach, go on, touch her."

"She is beautiful, real skinny, though. I kinda look like her, huh?"

I hear Carvin move to the opposite side of my bed, probably to give Zach more room to bond. "You all are twins. And, if you had met her prior to the accident, you would have met a woman who is loving, vibrant, smart, goofy, creative, and loves God. Just like you. She was, I mean she *is* dynamic, Zach." Sniffles follow Carvin's last few words as he attempts to fight back tears.

"Do you think she loved me, Mr. Carvin?" Zach slowly asks, as if afraid of what the answer may be.

My heart sinks. *More than I love myself.*

"Man, did she? Zach, she still loves you. Until the day she dies and beyond, you will always be her first love. Lord knows I wish you could hear her say it for yourself."

In the following moments of silence, I can feel their stares taking in every pore, every blemish, every skin cell gracing my body, searching for life. Their presence creates a peace I have never experienced until this very moment.

Lord, I just pray Zach understands my love for him.

"All right lil-man, we better head out; you have a flight to catch."

"Yeah, I know," Zach solemnly responds, "I just hate to leave her."

"I know."

"Mr. Carvin, is she going to die? You can be honest."

Carvin breaths in deeply, using his exhale to respond. "I don't know, lil-man. There is a chance God wants her in heaven more than we want her on earth. God, being God, always has the final say."

Stillness fills the room as we contemplate on the truth of Carvin's response.

God, is that it? Are you ready for me?

"You said she loves God, right? So, I kinda… Mr. Carvin, can I pray for her before we leave? I mean, I'm kinda not the best at praying, but I'm learning how to pray more at my summer Bible camp."

Zach is amazing. Only fourteen years old and he wants to pray for me. God, you have clearly answered my prayers. He is smart, loved, kind, strong, talented, and loves You. If You choose to take me to paradise today, I will be grateful because You have been so faithful to me, God. Who would have thought this day would come?

Before my thoughts could unravel into a full prayer, Carvin interrupts them.

"Of course! Ken and I prayed together all the time. One thing she loves is praying. To hear you pray, man, that would make her so happy, Zach."

I feel them grab my hands and move closer, Carvin on my right and Zachary on my left.

"Whenever you're ready, lil' man. When we talk to God, it doesn't have to be perfect, only sincere. Just speak from your heart."

"*Okay*, I'm ready. Um, kinda nervous," Zach stutters.

After a few moments of silence, Zach begins to pray a prayer that opens the gates of Heaven to summon me home. "Dear God and dear Jesus, um, thank you for allowing me to meet Ms. Kendall. Please bless her body and her heart. Let her know that I, um, that I thank her for giving me to the best parents in the world. I, um, I've been wanting to meet her and see her for a long time. And, um, I don't hate her, God. Please tell her I love her. I always will…" Zach pauses as he spirals into tears, however willing himself to continue. "God, I hope she will be with Your angels in heaven. Please tell her, um, please tell her to give G-ma and, um, Papa Earnest a hug for me. I hope she is not hurting. Ms. Kendall, if you can hear me, um, I love you and forgive you. You did the right thing. Thank you for that. In Jesus' name, Amen."

I've fallen in love all over again with you, Zachary.

He loves me. He forgives me. I recycle this through my mind multiple times, falling deeper and deeper into a love spell. He loves me. He forgives me. It's as if his words have whisked me away from my reality and I'm drifting through ethereal clouds of tranquility. Zachary is my greatest lesson gifted away. He was the purpose for my pain. As his prayer repeatedly sings to me, I feel the blood rush through every vein and the coolness of life splash against each pore.

So mesmerized by his words, I am unaware of their last kiss on the cheek and forever farewell. I do not sense my blood pressure dropping, pupils dilating, or hear the cardiac monitor flat lining. My ears are deaf to the chaotic flurry of nurses and doctors fighting to revive my heart. The melodic prayer of my first love serenades away every ounce of me. Anxious to halt my euphoria, Guilt rushes to distract me with memories of my past, but the Forgiveness of my son lessens its grip. The more I realize gifting Zachary away was my greatest legacy, the higher I ascend.

When I repeat his parting phrase in my mind, *I love you and forgive you*, the heavenly, regal chorus of one awakens my spirit, and the soothing voice calms my entire being. A delightful peace shines within me. For the first time in months, I open my eyes and experience all five senses as I take in the beauty surrounding me. For the first time in a long time, I hear my voice gently speak, "Hello."

"Hello, my precious daughter. Welcome home."

ABOUT THE AUTHOR

A vivacious California girl, Tiera Nacole received a Bachelor's of Science degree from Norfolk State University and a Master's of Public Health from Texas A&M University. She has extensive experience working in the medical arena, to include leadership, quality, and performance improvement.

A coach for women, men, and youth, Tiera has organized conferences and seminars centered around self-empowerment and life skills development. As the founder and president of the non-profit, Sisters Advocating Second Steps, she has created a network of individuals who collaborate monthly to impact and empower community members through a variety of service projects. Currently residing in Houston, Texas, she is working on producing a documentary and authoring her next novel.

Along with enjoying quality time with her family and friends, Tiera relishes in reading, dancing, meditating, exercising, eating, traveling, laughing, and gifting her heart away to those in need.

Let's Get Real

Thank you so much for reading *Lesson Gifted Away*! Regardless if you embarked on this journey alone or with a Book Club, please take some time to ponder the questions below. Keep it real!

1. Which Life Lesson(s) most resonated with you and why?

2. In what ways did Kendall adopt a victim mentality? How did it affect those closest to her?

3. What role did the personification of guilt play in Kendall Marie Johnson's life?

4. Can guilt and forgiveness coexist?

5. Do you believe Kendall should have told Carvin about the rape and/or adoption sooner? How would this have impacted their relationship?

6. What rights, if any, do you believe Carvin had in the fate of their unborn child? Does society support the rights of fathers?

7. Could Kendall's accident have been avoided? If so, how?

8. In what way(s) was Zachary Kendall's greatest lesson gifted away?

9. In what areas of your life are you giving guilt and/or shame too much control? What will you do to take back your power?

10. When you ponder your own life's journey, what has been your greatest life lesson so far? What are you doing to gift your lessons away to those around you?

If you know me, you know I truly value my readers. I would love to know your answers to the questions above and thoughts about *Lesson Gifted Away*. Let's connect via my website and/or social media.

In the meantime, continue to Live, Love, and gift away Lessons!

Website: www.tieranacole.com

Email: tieranacole@tieranacole.com

Instagram: @TieraNacole

Facebook: Tiera Nacole

CPSIA information can be obtained
at www.ICGtesting.com
Printed in the USA
FFOW03n1453150518
46583101-48626FF